MW01172542

HOMETOWN JUSTICE

Aftermath

Charles Cloninger

Kindle Direct Publishing

This book is dedicated to the friends who pushed me to continue the story, to the fans who silently cheer these characters on, and to the Vixen who made it all possible.

CONTENTS

AUTHOR'S NOTE

Greetings Everyone!

Welcome to the third installment of the Hometown Justice series. It's been a wild ride, huh? Since this journey began in Homecoming, our heroes have gone through some stuff, with even more stuff on the way. This note isn't to address any continuity errors from book two, this is to pre-warn you guys, the readers, that there are scenarios in this installment and future installments that may be deemed inappropriate for children under the age of 13 to read. Please use discretion when allowing smaller children to read the next installments.

As I mentioned in the previous Author's Note, these characters are based on people from my life, but I feel like I should point out that none of the events I write out have actually happened, nor do I wish them to happen to anyone. These events are strictly for plot and character development. I have done my absolute best to avoid all the details both here in this note and in the actual story, but for story purposes some of the details could not be ignored.

One more time, thank you all for the support.

Thank you all for allowing me to accomplish a childhood dream. Hometown Justice will wrap up its first arc officially with this story here, appropriately named Aftermath. Please enjoy.

Yours truly,
Charles Cloninger

CHAPTER ONE

The quaint little double wide on Double Shoals Road sat silent on the small acre lot. Its white exterior was starting to show age, but the home was obviously loved. Not a single light illuminated the yard, but one small bulb lit up the front room. The occupant of the home was busy planning her business spendings for the coming month. A light rain had started falling down, and that slowly turned to snow in the cold.

Headlights illuminated the home momentarily, before getting clicked off as the small black Honda pulled into the yard. The engine dies as the four doors open and five men climb out. The driver takes a long drag off his cigarette, extinguishing the fire and flicking the butt into the yard.

"Raymon, go around back. Dean, take the side door. Vaughn, Kaz, with me," the driver says in a hoarse whisper.

Two of the men, dressed in mechanics overalls, split away from the other three. The driver and the two remaining men walked gingerly up on the porch. The driver looked at the other two men, chuckles lightly before rapping on the wooden door with his knuckles three times.

"One second!" the female inside the home called out.

Moments later, she opens the door with a smile on her face.

"Tommy?" she asks, looking at the driver, "What brings you to these parts?"

"Just wanted to make sure there are no hard feelings between me and you, Toots," Tommy sneers, "and I need you to deliver a message to The Marine. Kaz, Vaughn, get her!"

Five hours later, Tommy drags the female outside in nothing but a robe using her vibrant red hair as a leash. Placing her limp body on a bench in the yard, Tommy kneels beside her while the other four men take turns emptying gas cans throughout the home, and all around the yard.

"You see, Alyson, I tried to warn everyone in this shithole town that I am not to be fucked with. I gave warning after warning after warning. No one would listen. I thought I had everyone's attention when I beat Kwondo and Manson in that tournament," Tommy clicks his tongue, "but then your buddy came back. The Marine has effectively taken the attention off of me and made everyone feel safe again," Tommy stretches a bit, "And now an example has to be made. I'm sorry it had to be you. You had a contract with me and you went and broke it,"

Alyson coughs, as tears stream down her cheeks. Her eyes have been swollen, her face bruised. She can barely breathe.

"I'm sorry, Toots, you say summat?" Tommy asks, lightning a cigarette and taking a drag off of it, "I know, I know, you were saving yourself for the Marine to get his shit straight and love you the way you two planned back in high school. But, tonight, me and my guys had to show you what a few real men are really like. Hope you enjoyed having all of us take turns on you," Tommy laughs, taking a deep breath and exhaling the smoke directly into Alyson's face, "I mean you were having so much fun, who could hear you say anything?"

"Y-You w-wont g-get a-away w-with t-this," Alyson barely manages to say, before a coughing fit takes over her.

"I think I already have princess. See, the guys are burning all the evidence right now. So you go ahead and send the signal that calls The Marine to your aid. You will be laying here warm and cozy while your hopes and dreams all burn up. Then when that nice little muscle car of his arrives, you can tell him that you were treated like a filthy whore by five men that he can't stand. See if he still wants you after that," Tommy laughs, spitting on Alyson, his saliva joining the other bodily fluids covering her face and the rest of her body. "If we get the urge later, slut, we will be back,"

Tommy gives a shrill whistle, pointing to the sky and making a circle over his head. Raymon drags a line of fuel over to Tommy, and blows a kiss to Alyson before climbing into the Honda. Tommy takes one final drag off his cigarette, flicking it into the line of fuel Ramon had dragged over to him. The cigarette ignites the fuel, creating a trail of flames that eventually ignite the double wide home, sending a large flame into the sky. Tommy and his crew speed off, leaving Alyson laying on the bench in the nude as the snow continues to fall.

Sirens wail in the distance as Alyson fades into unconsciousness.

CHAPTER TWO

'Fireman' by Lil Wayne breaks the eerie silence filling the Polkville Police Department. It was late, but Sheriff Alexander Ruler was still sitting at his desk when the phone began ringing. Looking at the caller ID, the Sheriff sees that the local Fire Chief is ringing him.

"Ruler," The Sheriff says, putting the call on speaker.

"Sheriff, we have a situation out here on Double Shoals Road," the calm collected voice of Fire Chief Matthew Cook comes through the speaker, "We were called out about a house fire. EMTs are on sight but the sole victim is refusing anything from anyone without speaking to you,"

"I'm on my way. Tell Alyson to give me ten," The Sheriff says, hanging up and running out the door.

Ten minutes later, a Police Cruiser pulls up to the smoldering remains of the once quaint, cozy home on the corner lot. Sheriff Alex Ruler steps from the patrol car and grabs his investigation pack. He immediately grabs surgical gloves and puts them on.

"Ruler," Matthew calls to him, snapping his attention to the left.

Sitting at the rear of the ambulance, Matthew is doing paperwork with Alyson on the stretcher. Alex approaches slowly, his eyes scanning everything. He could see signs of blunt force trauma, strangling, firm grips on Alyson's face, neck and forearms.

"What happened here?" Alex asks, as Jason hands him a clipboard.

"My full report will be on your desk at sun up. We needed you here so we could convince her to get to proper treatment. She's refusing anything without seeing you first," Matthew explains.

"Alyson, what happened?" Alex asks, turning to her on the stretcher.

"I dont remember how it began but I remember Tommy showing up on my doorstep before everything went down. Alex, promise me you wont do anything stupid," Alyson begs him, "Dont go to that compound. Dont lose your job as Sheriff over this,"

"Alyson, I swore to protect everyone in town. That includes you. Tommy will not get away with this," Alex says solemnly.

"I'm not even sure he was involved. He came by asking me to give you this," Alyson says, handing Alex a sealed envelope, "Something about the upcoming tournament,"

"He really may be innocent?" Alex asks.

"Possibly. I am still a little foggy on all the details. But if I remember something, you'll be the first I call," Alyson says.

Alex takes her hand in his, squeezing it gently. The EMTs load her up, as Alex turns to Matthew.

"Pretty bleak scene when we arrived. House was still burning with fifteen foot high flames. We found Alyson wrapped in a robe and nothing else when we got here. I called the EMTs, but she refused to talk to anyone until you got here," Matthew explains, "You want to investigate further?"

"Cause of the fire?" Alex asks, eyeballing the scene.

"Fuel Trails with a starter," Matthew says, "And this was the starter," Matthew holds up a ziplock bag with a cigarette inside, "Forensics could pull DNA and figure out who at least started the fire,"

"Thanks, Matt. Any other clues?" Alex asks, as another patrol car arrives and Tai climbs out.

"Just a footprint, that we can't take a good sample of due to the fallen snow," Matthew replies, "Maybe you can take a look at it?"

"Alex, what the hell happened?" Tai asks, joining Alex and Matthew.

"We aren't sure yet, Kwondo. Has anyone else gotten a call?" Alex asks.

"Ken, but he's covering my class so I could be here for you. Jones is manning the dispatch station," Tai explains, "Manson was worried about you going all feral tiger and hunting down whoever did this,"

"Makes sense. We only have one piece of evidence, though Tai. Alex doesn't really have enough to go feral with?" Matthew chuckles, "Besides, we have proven he is beyond what he used to do as a teen,"

"The footprint is over here," Matthew leads the two officers towards the bench where Alyson was found "Whoever did this, crouched here beside Alyson. The imprint is deeper than it should be, just not clear enough to make a cast with all this snow,"

"I have an idea," Alex says, taking out his phone and snapping a few pictures at different angles, "Now to send these over to Kenji, and wait for his call," Alex is interrupted by his phone ringing, "Ruler! Yeah, Kenji, I need your forensics team to analyze those pics and get me the footprint? Think it can happen? Sweet. Meet me at the Police Station in three hours,"

"You really going to trust Keith's team?" Tai asks.

"I mean his team has technology out the whazoo," Alex replies.

"Right, I forgot about that," Tai says, "Are we 100% certain this wasn't a random act though?"

"Fuel lines ran into the house, and were ignited with a cigarette," Matthew explains, "the fire started outside. This wasn't random. If it were, every other home on this block would be on fire,"

"And whoever did it, did a serious number on Alyson. She was beaten, bruised, and possibly raped," Alex admits, "Speaking of which, Kwondo, you go back to the police station. Matthew, if you find anything else, reach out. I'm going to the hospital to talk to Alyson if she is able too,"

"Be careful Ruler," Tai calls as the three men part ways.

"Careful is my middle name, Tai," Alex chuckles climbing into his car.

****

Tommy Leons sat in his office, looking at the scene unfold on his computer. Unbeknownst to everyone there, Tommy had hidden a camera near Alyson's house. He had no audio, but he could watch everything unfold. Sipping on his wine, Tommy laughs to himself. *The Marine answered the call. Soon, he will know the true extent of my power*, Tommy thinks looking down at his right wrist. The metallic silver wrist watch with a spinning dial face beamed back up at him. The Relic System had been designed for him by a team of scientists. It would allow him to once more tap into the natural rei of his body, since his had been sealed away when he was a child. Tommy loved the feeling of the rei flowing through his body. The drawbacks of the system had been flushed recently, and Tommy had received the upgraded version.

"Boss," a male voice called, interrupting his thoughts, "You have a phone call on line two. Bertinelli,"

"Thank you, Marcus," Tommy says, picking up his phone, "Mr. Bertinelli, a pleasure,"

There was a long moment of silence, as Tommy listened to Mr. Bertinelli speak, taking a few notes as he listened.

"Mr. Bertinelli, I will take care of this matter. Thank you for bringing it to my attention," Tommy exhales slowly, "I will send a message, that no one in town will ever forget,"

****

Alex approaches the nurse desk at Shelby Hospital. The nurse behind the desk smiles at him as she stands up.

"How can I help you Sheriff?"

"Well," Alex leans over and reads her name tag, "Emily, I'd like to see Alyson Jergens Please?"

"Jergens? She's in room 414," The nurse explains, pointing down the hallway to the left.

"Emily, I need a huge favor. Anyone who doesn't have a sheriff's badge or a Kwondo's School Badge cannot enter her room? Can you set that up for me?" Alex asks.

"Can you provide a copy of the School badge?" Emily asks, extending her right hand.

"There ya go. Thank you so much. It is imperative that no one but those with the right badges speak to Alyson," Alex says, dropping a Kwondo school crest badge into her palm.

Alex leaves the nurses desk and heads towards Alyson's room. He softly knocks before pushing the door open. Alyson is laying in her bed, with the room lights dimmed. Alex clears his throat, startling her.

"Didn't mean to scare, ya," He says sheepishly. "How are you doing?"

"I'm in the hospital, Alex. How do you think I'm doing?" Alyson snaps back, but the tone is friendly enough that he catches the hint.

"I am so sorry this happened to you. I'm going to do everything in my power to get the culprit. But I'm going to need your help," Alex explains, "I need you to give me all the details you can remember about what happened,"

"I was doing order management for the diner, paying bills, and sorting through employee files that Eric Watts had maintained in the last fifteen years. There was a knock at the door. I answered it, and Tommy was standing there with his friends, Mark Kaz and Matt Vaughn," Alyson explains.

"Tommy showed up at your house with the twins? I thought they were his hired muscles," Alex says, writing the info down in a notepad, "Sorry, Alyson, what next?"

"I invited Tommy in. I didn't invite in the twins. I offered him tea, and food. I went back to work as we talked. He spoke about some tournament coming up and asked me to convince you to enter,"

"Anything else?" Alex asks, writing all this information down.

"I remember smelling gasoline, and seeing two other men out in the yard but I dont know who they were," Alyson replies.

"Do you remember what these other two men were doing? If I did a line up, could you point them out?" Alex asks.

"They were pouring something from red canisters. I couldn't tell what it was. But I remember Tommy saying he was going to be leaving. He opened the door, walked outside but the twins came inside. Alex, what happened next, I'm ashamed to tell you," Alyson begins to cry.

"Hey, easy. Nothing to worry about," Alex reassures her to the best of his abilities, "Alyson, I already have a pretty good idea of what happened. And if I'm right, what happened changes nothing between us. It doesnt change how I feel, and it never will,"

"Alex, Tommy, Kaz, Vaughn, and those other two guys....they...they....violated me, they made me feel worthless and disgusting. We joked and said Tommy was just like the guys who ran the dojo with the snake logo, but he is so much worse. Tommy is terrifying when he wants to be," Alyson cries.

Alex takes her hand into his. He wipes tears from her cheeks and smiles.

"Don't worry. I won't let him get away with this," he says softly, "You focus on getting well," Alex kisses her cheek softly, "You will be under restrictions until released from the hospital. No one can come see you without a sheriff's badge or a Kwondo School Badge,"

"Where are you going?" Alyson asks, as Alex stands up.

"To do my job. I'm going to interrogate Leons and his crew," Alex says fiercely.

****

Stepping out of the hospital, Alex takes his phone from the clip on his belt. Scrolling through the contacts, he sighs deeply before pressing the call button on the name 'Tiffani'. Three rings and suddenly he hears, "Hello?"

"Tiffani?" Alex asks in confusion.

"Speaking," the voice on the other end replies, "Is this Bobby Drake?"

"No, no. This is Gunnery Sergeant Alexander Graham Ruler. I'm seeking Staff Sergeant Tiffani Jergens?"

"Alex? What happened?" Tiffany yells, causing Alex to hold the phone away from his ear.

"Tiff, calm down. I just need to know how to contact your parents," Alex says.

"No, Ruler, you tell me what happened," Tiffany says.

"Alyson was assaulted, physically, mentally, emotionally, and sexually by Leons. I need to let your parents know so I can give them the proper badges to get in to see her," Alex explains, "So while your parents are sitting with Alyson, I'm going after Tommy,"

"Alex, my parents are unreachable at the moment, doing some work for the church overseas. I'm on the next flight out, I'll meet you at the airport outside of Polkville. Just you, no one else," Tiffany says.

"Text me arrival details and I'll be there," Alex sighs, as the line goes dead.

****

Tommy marches into the garage of the casino. Vince Raymon and Chris Dean are working on separate vehicles when he walks in, followed by Marcus wheeling himself into the four bay garage.

"Someone, anyone, explain to me why the actual fuck I have four bays, and only two have vehicles in them? Vehicles that I need on the road before the end of the week?" Tommy bellows, causing the two mechanics to jump up, hitting their heads.

"Tommy," Vince exclaims, "Since we fired Mitchell, we haven't had the time to do the extra work, what with burning the bitch's house down and shit,"

"I need these vehicles up and running before the weekend, no excuses," Tommy spits, "Or you can consider yourselves demoted to civilian and not part of my vision,"

"Tommy," Chris says, "You have us doing so much extra stuff, there aint no way. In this vehicle alone, I have to recalibrate the transmission to match up to the new engine specs,"

"Then what the fuck am I paying you to actually do?" Tommy seethes, getting right in Dean's face, their noses almost touching, " You claimed you was the best fucking diesel mechanic in the whole fucking state. And yet, you can't get four vehicles up to spec in less than a week? Bagwell, it looks like we fired the wrong fucking mechanic,"

"Tommy, its not like that at all. You've just had Raymon and I doing other jobs and we haven't exactly spent more than an hour in the garage," Chris shoots back, "It was a situation where we had to choose whether or not to listen to you and lose our job or complete the jobs in here and deal with the backlash,"

"Look, Boss, I ain't agreeing with anything this little pissant says, but I'm agreeing with the fact we ain't had a whole lot of time in the garage," Raymon says, "If you need these vehicles finished by the end of the week, you need to leave us in the fucking garage,"

"Listen, you spitfuck, I have other business to attend too, but when I get back, the three of us, will have a discussion concerning both of your futures with this company," Tommy seethes, "Bagwell, get the twins and lets go,"

Marcus removes his phone and dials a number, mutters something into the phone, and moments later a sleek black Nissan Sentra pulls up. The windows are heavily tinted, and it appears to be covered in bullet proof armor. The driver's side door opens, and one of the twins steps out, at the same time as the passenger's side door opens and the other twin steps out. Tommy walks to the passenger's side, and steps into the front seat. Mark Kaz pushes the door closed, while Matt Vaugh helps Marcus into the back seat, folding up Bagwell's wheelchair and putting it in the trunk. Tommy takes the driver's seat as everyone else piles into the Sentra.

"Damn it, Kaz, you forgot to fill the tank up. I gotta stop by DeRisi's and get fuel," Tommy says, steering the car towards the Gas and Go Station.

Tommy pulls the sleek black car up to the pump outside DeRisi's Gas and Go. He gets out of the car, puts the fuel nozzle in the tank and starts the pump. He hands fifty dollars to one of the twins.

"Get whatever you guys want. You have ten minutes. NO CORNNUTS!" Tommy yells, as he walks towards the garage, looking at the fuel prices as he does.

Tommy approaches the mechanic beneath a camaro. Without a word, Tommy lowers the hydraulic jack so that Bobby DeRisi was trapped beneath the camaro.

"Bobby De-Fuckin'-Risi" Tommy seethes, "I thought we had ourselves a deal. You keep the gas prices lowered, and I keep making you rich. Wanna explain what happened?"

"T-Tommy! I-I cant breathe!!" Bobby gasps.

"Oh bullshit, DeRisi, if you can talk you can breathe," Tommy taunts, "I think you have already been given two warnings about double crossing me, DeRisi,"

Bobby DeRisi manages to reach into his pocket and hit a silent alarm button. Tommy is unaware of this as he continues to talk to DeRisi.

"It looks like I need to make an example out of you and everyone else involved with my operations. DeRisi, I really enjoyed being your partner in crime, but it appears as if it's time for us to part ways, our agreement is over," Tommy kicks over a barrel of gasoline DeRisi had in the garage and walks away, leaving DeRisi beneath the car trapped as the gasoline slowly leaks from the barrel.

Tommy returns to his vehicle and removes the fuel nozzle from the tank. He drops it on the ground with the handle still leaking gasoline everywhere. Tommy removes his confederate flag lighter with his initials etched into the steel and lights a cigarette. The twins both climb into the car as Tommy starts the engine and rings a donut in the parking lot, tossing his zippo lighter out the window, still lit. The lighter ignites the fuel and causes an explosion as Leons drives towards Shelby, leaving DeRisi's in a smoldering ruin.

CHAPTER THREE

The entire town felt the rumble of DeRisi's blowing up. There was only a matter of time before Jason and the fire department had surrounded the area doing their job of fighting the flames. Tai and Ken arrived after Jason called the department in.

"Where's Alex?" Matthew asks, as Tai approaches.

"On assignment elsewhere. What do you have for us?" Tai inquires, "What happened here?"

"Unsure of anything concrete except for the obvious," Matthew says, "But we know it started at the fuel pump with this,"

Matthew holds up a ziplock bag with a burnt zippo lighter inside. Ken removes a pair of blue plastic gloves from a pocket on his belt. Putting the gloves on, Ken takes the bag from Jason and examines it closely.

"I can't make out the initials on the side, but it definitely has a confederate flag on one side of the lighter," Ken says, "Good looking out, Cook. What else do we know? Casualties?"

"Approximately seven dead, at least ten injured," Matthew explains, "I have no clue what happened but it was big,"

"Okay. I'll get the crime scene team on it," Tai sighs,

"We can start gathering information and clues,"

"Good," Matthew says, "I'm supposed to be golfing today, but alas, here I am,"

Tai calls Keith.

"Nakamura," Keith answers.

"Keith, its Tai. How fast can you get your forensic team together? We have a huge case that we need forensic specialists to look at. I'm at DeRisi's Gas and Go or what's left of it," Tai asks.

"Give me twenty minutes. I'll come gather evidence and get the rest of my team on it," Keith replies.

"Would you mind showing me what you consider evidence so I know what to look for?" Tai asks.

"Of course," Keith says, "Hey, uh, did you do a rei scan?"

"Yeah, Ken is doing it right now," Tai replies, "It's coming up a bust,"

"So whoever did this isn't able to manipulate rei," Keith sighs, "Do you see anything that is out of place?"

"You mean like the nozzle to the fuel pump that is no longer standing?" Tai asks.

"Yes. That is evidence, bag and tag it," Keith says, "I'm almost there,"

****

"Special Agent Casey Elkins?" Alex asks, as a petite dark haired female approaches him.

She is wearing a very form fitting kevlar uniform that is dark blue in color, with many pockets. The letters RIPD written across her shoulders and right chest. Alex is stunned by the look of her hazel eyes over her mirrored sunglasses.

"The very one. Regional Investigation of Preternatural Crimes Division Special Agent Casey

Elkins," she says, her voice as soft and sweet as the angel she was.

Alex could feel his heart in his throat. He awkwardly opened the police cruiser door, and beckoned her inside.

"Sheriff Cooper instructed me to give you a tour, but we just got a call for an explosion in town. Would you like to ride along? Or should I allow the deputies to handle this?" Alex asks.

"Do I look like some pansy ass princess?" Elkins asks, raising an eyebrow, "I'd love to investigate,"

"Well lets blow this popsicle stand," Alex says, as Elkins climbs into the passenger's seat of his cruiser, allowing Alex to close the door.

Moments later, Alex and Casey arrive at what remains of DeRisi's Gas and Go. Tai and Ken approach the vehicle as Alex and Casey step out of it.

"Deputies. This is Special Agent Casey Elkins. She is visiting Polkville for a few days and wanted to watch us in action. What do we have?" Alex asks.

"We've got two pieces of evidence, but no solid leads, yet. Chief Cook informed us the fire started here, lit by a cigarette," Tai explains, "I've called Keith, he's on his way with his forensics team,"

"Ruler," Casey says, "From what I've read on you, you are able to sense rei, correct?"

"Yes. The three of us standing here are pretty skilled in sensing, creating, and manipulating rei," Alex replies, "Why do you ask?"

"Open your sixth sense, read the rei," Casey explains, "Tell me what you see,"

Simultaneously, Alex, Tai, and Ken did as Casey suggested, as their own natural rei spread from their bodies and coated the area of the explosion.

"The explosion didn't happen at the gas pump. The fire was lit here, and it traveled along the path of the spilt fuel to the garage, where presumably, Bobby DeRisi had an abundance of fuel stored, which caused the explosion," Tai gasps, "Meaning whoever did this has it out for the owner of the business,"

"Who owns DeRisi's other than Bobby DeRisi?" Ken asks, rubbing his chin.

"Well, Sheriff, I've got one more thing to throw on your plate. We can't get answers out of Bobby, we just id'd his body. Trapped beneath a car he was working on," Matthew explains.

"Ruler," Keith says as he arrives, "Evidence that has been bagged for me?"

"Tai will handle that, Keith. Say, is Aidan in town?" Alex asks hopefully.

"Unfortunately, Ruler, I can neither confirm nor deny that," Keith says as he walks past Alex, Casey, and Ken.

"Ken, can you try to track down the owner of DeRisi's Gas and Go," Alex says, pinching his nose, "You see, Casey, this is what happens whenever you leave home for eleven years and come back. EVERYTHING changes,"

"Trust me, don't I know. Recruited straight out of high school due to my rei abilities by RIPD. Taken away to be trained by their arctic base," Casey explains, "Been away from Blacksburg ever since. That's why I was chosen for this region, I know it better"

"Wait, there are actually undead beings?" Alex asks.

"Around half the planet belongs to the undead. We are talking about vampires, demons, variants, and other non-humans species mixed in with the undead. Anyways, Ruler, I went to the Preternatural Collage, trained with some of the best, graduated top of my class, and was recruited by The RIPD. I've been away from home almost as long as you were. I'm returning after ten years. But Sheriff Cooper wanted me to meet with you because you are able to control rei," Casey explains, "This means the recent rise of rei based crimes called for a Specialist, and I need to know who is on my side and who isn't,"

"You do realize that as officers of the law, right and wrong are morally gray, right?" Alex asks, "Because what you may consider wrong, the guy committing the crime may think he is justified in doing so,"

"Yes, and that's why I'm coming home to handle things. I'm charged with policing the Carolinas but my first act as the Regional Detective is to discover what is happening to the people in my hometown of Blacksburg. Thrush seems to be the culprit but I have no idea where it is coming from," Casey explains herself.

"Maybe stick around here for a few days and see if we can locate some thrush here in Polkville. As close as Blacksburg is, I'm sure someone in Polkville is doing the drug," Alex suggests, "Plus, I'd love to actually hear more about your actual job description,"

"Only if I get to be involved with the investigation," Casey smirks, "And I'll need a place to sleep,"

"I got you covered. We can talk to Skooter and get you a room at El Rancho Del Skooter," Alex smirks.

"Do all small towns have a local bar with a motel in the town?" Casey asks, as the two new found friends ventured back to Alex's cruiser, "Blacksburg has one too, called Byars Bar and Chill,"

****

"You blew up our number one fuel dispenser and drug provider," Bertinelli asks calmly, "Mr. Leons, would you kindly explain why?"

Bertinelli was on the holoscreen in Tommy's office.

Antoine DeMarco was there too. Both men were furious with Tommy, but wanted to hear his reasoning. Tommy shuffled his feet a bit. He closed his right fist tightly.

"Bertinelli, DeMarco, I'm not going to ask either of you to understand why I did what I did. I'm going to ask you to bare with me while I attempt to explain my reasoning for the betterment of the business," Tommy says softly, in his calmest voice.

"We are listening, gringo," Antoine growls.

"Mr. Leons, in our industry, time is money. Do not waste either of mine," Bertinelli explains.

Tommy brings his left wrist to chest level, allowing the light from the projectors to reflect off the face of his watch. He rotated the face plate, until the number on the screen started increasing. When the face plate reads 100, Tommy flexes his arms as his shirt disintegrates under the pure pressure of the flowing rei escaping Tommy's body.,

"I have perfected the relic system. I can one hundred percent control my rei now with 100% access to it," Tommy explains, manipulating rei in his hands to showcase his control, "There are no drawbacks at this point in the research. No stamina drain, no time limit, nothing,"

"I'm sorry, Mr. Leons, but this has nothing to do with what happened to DeRisi's Gas and Go," Bertinelli states.

"It has everything to do with what happened to DeRisi's Gas and Go," Tommy smirks, "I'm entering the Strongest Under The Heavens Tournament. I'm going to defeat Ruler and Kincaid. I'm going to prove to you that I am worth every penny you have spent on me," Tommy says, "DeRisi was piggybacking money from you, Bertinelli, and you DeMarco. 1.25 Million a month, drained into an offshore account,"

"And I was under the impression you had stopped this," Bertinelli laughs.

"I did. But DeRisi was a sneaky sum bitch. He continued pulling money from us. I put a stop to it finally by eliminating the entire store from the face of the map. Now Ruler is investigating the cause of it, which prevents him from training for the tournament." Tommy explains, "And with his attention on the investigation, I am taking my training to the next level with a new prototype, fresh off the presses. A weighted training room," Tommy explains, "DeRisi left behind this weighted training room and I'm going to utilize it in preparation for defeating the Marine,"

"Why does this require the explosion?" Bertinelli asks.

"Are you deaf in your old age, 'Dad'?" Tommy asks, his words like poison, "The Marine will be focused on solving the investigation of who done the crime, while I'm preparing for our inevitable fight in the tournament you are so graciously hosting,"

"Haven't you already lost a football game to the Marine?" Bertinelli asks, without flinching.

"Yes, but this is a new venue for me to overthrow the Marine," Tommy says.

"Gringo, you are putting too much effort into defeating the Marine," Antoine says, "You should just go into his house and kill him while he sleeps,"

"Where is the fun in that?" Tommy asks, "Besides, if both of you gentlemen would check your Relic Systems, you would see that I am currently performing at a ratio higher than that of the Marine, and I plan to get stronger,"

"You've become obsessed, Leons," Antoine says, "When you fail, me and The Wendigos will take care of the Marine and resume control of this town,"

"You only wish you and your Wendigos could take control of this town," Tommy laughs, "**Fist Style!**

Cobra Fang Blade!" Tommy cups his hand as if holding a cylinder and nothing happens at first.

DeMarco chuckles before white lightning cackles around his hand, erupting into a twisted blade of rei. Tommy brandishes the weapon of pure rei with expert precision and skill. Demonstrating his new found abilities to Bertinelli and Antoine.

"This is my new technique. The first of many to come. And unlike the Marine, I can make this weapon and utilize it in the middle of combat," Tommy explains, "So, Sensei, I come before you, offering my Cobra Fang Blade as your personal weapon, to kill the Marine in your tournament. Grant me the ability to skip straight to the Semi-Finals,"

"Douglas Kincaid is getting seeded straight to the Finals. I suppose you could get seeded straight to the Semi-Finals," Bertinelli sighs before Tommy interrupts, "Sir, I would like to fight Kincaid before I fight the Marine,"

"Kincaid wants to fight the marine as well," Bertinelli explains, "How about this, if the two of you can best each other, the winner gets the Marine. I will make sure you both face other in the semi-finals,"

"Sounds fair," Tommy agrees, "DeMarco, are you entering anyone from your Wendigo School?"

"No, Vato. Wendigos aren't going to partake this year. We lost so badly last year, we are going to take a year off to perfect our new fighting techniques," Antoine says, "Besides, I wouldn't want to be the reason you didnt get your grudge match with the Marine or Kincaid,"

"Smart move, Antoine, There is a reason we work well as partners and make believe rivals," Tommy smiles.

"Mr. Leons, I will put everything into motion for you, get stronger and pray The Marine doesn't find your most recent supply of Thrush," Bertinelli sighs deeply, "Now that I have your attention though, my connections have warned me of a Special Agent being sent to the Carolinas on the look for anything preternatural, including but not limited too rei manipulators, form altering drugs," Bertinelli says, his fingertips touching.

"Form Altering Drugs? So someone in the Preternatural Department knows about Thrush having that transformation ability?" Antoine asks.

"Transformation ability? I'm more worried about the rei manipulators. What does this mean for The Relic System?" Tommy says.

"Do not fret, Leons, I did not deliver a transformative Thrush into your hands. I knew doing so would lead to us being discovered," Antoine snickers.

"Gentlemen. The Preternatural Department is only active due to the recent rise of rei users in this area. They aren't investigating anything at the moment, but we must prevent them from catching onto our organization," Bertinelli reminds, "Leons, keep the rei usage down during this tournament. Do not let them defeat you,"

"Have you checked your Rei Gauge? I'm undefeatable now," Tommy boasts.

"You still haven't beaten the Marine," Antoine says, slyly.

"I defeated his two friends with the imperfect Relic System. I can defeat him with the perfected version," Tommy retorts, "I'm going to begin training and mastering a new maneuver to utilize against Kincaid, Leons Out,"

With the press of a button, Tommy closes the images of both men on his wall. With his rei flared around him, Tommy lit up the darkness like a flashlight. Rage filled him, as he pointed to the screen that once had Antoine's face.

"I'll show you!" Tommy yells, as a thin beam of

rei erupts from his fingertip, burning a neat hole in the center of the screen, before ricocheting around the small room. Tommy ducked it three times, amazed at the color of the rei traveling around the room, "I think I'll call it the Lethal Beam," Tommy chuckles, "And I can control it very slightly,"

"With training, you will be able to do more than control it slightly," a voice says from the doorway.

Tommy turns to see a tall, older man standing in the shadows, smoking a cigarette. Tommy instinctively goes for his gun, but the man standing before him exhales a large quantity of smoke.

"You act without thinking, but can you think without acting?" the man's voice asks, as Tommy fires his gun three times at three different targets.

"Who the hell are you?" Tommy shouts.

"I am the originator of the Way of The Fist in the Carolinas. I taught your stepfather everything he knows and apparently he taught you," the man snarls before grabbing Tommy by the neck and knocking the gun from his hands, "Except how to fight a more experienced fighter,"

"WHO THE HELL ARE YOU?" Tommy growls between gritted teeth, struggling to breath.

"My name is Joseph Bailey. I brought the Way of The Fist into the Carolinas back in the 70s, before Yoshimoto Kwondo brought his defense only bullshit to the Carolinas. I can help you win, and I can train you in ways you've never imagined," Tommy heard whispered in his ear, "I just want to help you,"

"Help me? You attacked me!" Tommy replies.

"I struck first. The first most basic rule of the Way of The Fist," Joseph explains, releasing Tommy, shoving him forward. "Unlike you, I don't need rei to overpower my opposition. I've been doing this since before Kwondo came to the carolinas. Since before rei was introduced to the world of martial arts,"

"Thanks for the information," Tommy smirks, firing off two of his newly acquired Lethal Beams beams at Joseph.

Shockingly, Joseph captured the beams in his two open palms and caused them to fizzle out, ceasing their existence. He chuckles slightly.

"Just because I have no need for rei, doesn't mean I have no idea how to combat the stuff. I can manipulate it too, just not as well in my old age," Joseph explains, "I'm no stranger to the ancient art of rei, but I dislike relying on it. With the right, training, you too could be as dangerous as me,"

"What if I don't want your help?" Tommy bellows.

"Then I won't help you. Your choice, I'll be around," Joseph says, reaching into his shirt pocket and removing a business card from it, "Give me a call when you want to stop being a pussy," Joseph flicks the card at Tommy with precision.

The card floats through the air and lands perfectly in Tommy's hand.

"That's Rei Control for you, kid," Joseph laughs, turning to walk away.

"Wait! I'll take your lessons. You only get three weeks," Tommy says.

"Three weeks will get you the absolute basics taught. But it will make you strong enough to outlast your opponents in a tournament setting. Deal," Joseph explains, "I just require room and food,"

"I think this can be arranged," Tommy says, "When do we start?"

"Tomorrow morning, 4:30 am. Corner of Stagecoach and Ruler Farm Road. Don't fret, we will be far enough away from your enemy's house for him to see anything. Do not eat or drink anything before you arrive," Joseph says.

"Can I bring my men? Or are you only agreeing to train me?" Tommy asks.

"Bring as many as you want, but no food or drink before arriving. No coffee. The training will wake you up enough," Joseph says, turning to leave.

CHAPTER FOUR

Three Weeks until Tournament

Tommy Leons had never been pushed this far in any type of training regimen he had ever endured. Joseph Bailey was making them hurt in places they didn't know they had. Tommy had gathered Brutus, Chris Dean, and Vince Raymon to join him in the training. All four men were sweating before 5 am. Joseph had made them run from the corner of Ruler Farm Road and Stagecoach Trail all the way through Polkville, to the Fallstone city limits sign, and run back. Once they reached the vehicles, He immediately had them begin their training with twenty five traditional push ups, twenty five traditional sit ups, and twenty five traditional jumping jacks before pushing them into another long distance run.

"This will eliminate your body's need for stamina usage. Push it until it is too tired to move. Then push it further. Once we complete this run, we will drive back to the training facility I have rented out in Shelby, and we will push beyond those limitations," Joseph called out to the four men he was training.

Once the men were in Shelby at the training

facility, Joseph had them doing very unorthodox training methods: handstand pushups, walking across hot coals and broken glass, weight lifting with car parts along with traditional training like a football team would go through.

"Someone," Tommy gasps for breath, "explain to me why," Tommy dry heaves, "this guy thinks torture is training?"

"Probably because it's the same thing his sensei did to him?" Chris says before he dry heaves as well, "I-I can't take this anymore. Leons, I'm not a fighter. I'm a diesel mechanic,"

"Don't tell me that you pussies are calling it quits already?" Joseph asks, walking over.

For the first time, since meeting the man, Tommy finally got a good look at him. Joseph's graying hair was cut short, in a military style. His gray eyes had seen war, and while it appeared as though Joseph was blind in his left eye due to the way the eye seemed to be glazing over, Tommy could tell that Joseph saw everything going on. The jagged scar across his check reminded Tommy of a large crooked snake. Joseph stood taller than Tommy, who stood roughly five feet eight inches tall.

"No sir. Water break, Dehydration is a killer," Vince replies, as Tommy was still busy dry heaving.

"Good. Take ten minutes, and we will then go into actual combat practices," Joseph smirks, taking a flask from his inner coat pocket and sipping it.

"Combat practices? We are extremely exhausted, and you want us to fight?" Brutus asks, "I don't know if you know this, sir, but I am the only person on this team who uses Psyjicc Energy, and if I try to go into a fight without full stamina, my energy devours my body," Brutus explains.

"Then I guess you aren't up to snuff. Get out of this dojo," Joseph yells, "You aren't Way of The Fist material,"

"Not Way of The Fist Material? You son of a bitch, I am the only person who has trained under The Way of The Fist that has stood a fight against The Marine and lived to tell the tale," Brutus bellows.

"Psyjicc energy has always been a joke, and will always be a joke. No one utilizes that in an actual fight," Joseph says, "I tell you what, big man. You get a full day's rest, rebuild your stamina, and then you and I will fight. If you win, you have proven that you are Way of The Fist Material and I will give you three hundred dollars. If I win, you leave this dojo and you no longer work for Leons?" Joseph looks at Tommy, "And no one is to give him any advice on my skills,"

"You bastard. I accept," Brutus says, as he storms out of the dojo.

"All I can say, Joseph, is Brutus isn't fired if he loses. He is my strongest fighter," Tommy coughs.

"After I finish with you three here today, you would do best to reevaluate your employees fighting skills," Joseph says, "Not get your asses back to training,"

Joseph walks out of the room.

****

"Commander," Keith begins, entering Alex's office with a file folder, before seeing Alex and Casey sitting behind Alex's desk, "Oh. Whoa, I didn't expect you to have female companionship,"

"This isn't what it looks like, Kenji. This is Special Agent Casey Elkins, and she was looking over the files I have on the drug Thrush," Alex states, "Casey, this is Former NCIS Agent Keith Nakamura a.k.a Kenjiro a.k.a Kenji,"

"Pleasure to meet you," Casey says, "is this your forensics guy?"

"My Forensics guy, my stealth attacker, and one of

my closest friends I made in the service," Alex looks at the folder in Keith's hand, "What ya got there?"

"This? This is everything I found using the evidence gathered at DeRisi's. Wanna go over it?" Keith asks.

"Sure, have a seat. Casey is assisting me on this case," Alex explains.

"Something Preternatural about the case?" Keith raises his eyebrow, "Because my evidence doesn't suggest anything Preternatural,"

"We aren't sure yet, Mr. Nakamura, but Sheriff Ruler's mechanic uncovered Thrush in Tommy Leons' truck he had impounded a few days ago, which is a drug of interest in my department," Casey explains.

"Okay, so my evidence links Tommy to the explosion of the Gas'N'Go," Keith explains, taking a picture from the manilla folder, "This was the key item,"

Alex takes the picture and looks at it. The picture depicts a burnt zippo lighter with a confederate flag on the side and the letters TL etched into the casing of it.

"Tommy's lighter?" Alex asks, "How does this link Tommy? He could have dropped it in the parking lot prior to the explosion,"

"Because I also found video evidence against him too. Kenta set up cameras around the town right after you were elected as Sheriff, and two of them covers DeRisi's. Take a look," Keith says, pointing to the monitors in the corner.

"Kenta never showed me how to operate that shit. Hang on though, I can get Officer Jones in here," Alex smiles, grabbing his walkie, "Officer Jones, can you come into my office please?"

"Sure thing, Sheriff," Jones replies.

"That dude is way too cheerful," Keith sighs, causing Casey to chuckle.

"Keith, he survived a scary ordeal, man. Cut him

some slack," Alex says softly, "And if you guys hadn't intervened, he probably wouldn't have survived,"

"So he gets a second chance on life, and he decides to use it as a way to annoy everyone who hates cheerful people before their sixth cup of coffee or twelfth cup of Jim?" Keith asks.

"They allow you to drink in your line of work?" Casey asks.

"I do as I please, lady," Keith blows the hair out of his eyes.

"Run that by me again, Lieutenant?" a voice says from the doorway.

"Casey, this is Corporal Larry "Kurokon" Armstrong," Alex introduces the newcomer before Casey interrupts him.

"You are Psychosis?" she exclaims.

"Depends on who you ask," Larry responds.

"I'm 100% certain. That's how you earned the nickname, Kurokon. It's a rough translation to Psychosis in a ancient language that no one remembers but you," Casey exclaims, "You are the RIPD's largest target,"

"Target? The RIPD has a most wanted list?" Alex asks.

"Okay," Casey chuckles, "Let me backup, when I say target I mean high profile suspects in the sudden increase of rei activity,"

"Agent Elkins, my dear, I think you are just feeding my ego too much. We both know I am no rei user," Larry chuckles,

"Keith, did you really tell the lady that you do as you please? Not on my watch you don't,"

"What brings you in, Kuro?" Alex asks.

"Just thought I'd stop in on my way through town. I didn't get the memo that we were working on a case with RIPD," Larry chuckles.

"Casey is aiding with the current case of the

explosion at DeRisi's. She thinks that there might an some involvement with Tommy and his people," Alex explains.

Larry chuckled, leaning against the doorframe. "Well, well, well. Looks like you've stumbled onto something big here, Alex. And you've even got the RIPD interested. Color me intrigued."

Officer Jones arrives, and Alex explains to him what he requires with the video system. Matt pulls up the video requested and allows the team to view it.

Alex sighed, rubbing his temples. "Look, we're still trying to put all the pieces together. But if Tommy's involved, and this Thrush drug is in play, I've got a bad feeling things are gonna escalate quickly."

Casey nodded, her hazel eyes serious. "Sheriff Ruler's right. If there's a preternatural angle to this case, we need to act fast. The RIPD's intel suggests there could be some dangerous players converging on Polkville for this tournament."

Keith raised an eyebrow. "Dangerous how? Like 'rip a man's spine out' dangerous or 'blow up a gas station' dangerous? Because it looks like we might have both on our hands."

"Exactly," Alex said grimly. "Which is why we need to split up and cover more ground. Keith, you and your team keep digging into the forensics. Look for anything tying Tommy directly to the attack on Alyson and the explosion."

Keith nodded, already making mental notes.

Alex turned to Casey. "Agent Elkins, you said the RIPD has files on known rei users? It's time to crack those open and see if any of our suspects have popped up on your radar before."

"On it," Casey confirmed. "I'll loop in my contacts, see if they can give us any additional intel on what might be coming our way."

Finally, Alex looked at Larry, a wry smile tugging at his mouth. "Guess that leaves you and me to go knock on some doors, Kuro. Between your knack for reading people and my stellar diplomatic skills, we ought to be able to shake something loose."

Larry smirked. "Diplomatic? That what they're calling it these days? Works for me, boss. I've been itching to have a friendly chat with Leons anyway."

Alex clapped his hands together. "Alright then, we've all got our marching orders. Let's get to work, people. The clock's ticking and I don't plan on letting this powder keg blow up in our faces. Meeting adjourned."

As the team filed out, Alex couldn't shake the feeling that this was just the tip of the iceberg. But one way or another, he'd get to the bottom of it. Polkville was his town to protect, and he'd be damned if he let it go down in flames on his watch...

****

Casey stepped out of the police station, pulling her phone from her pocket. The crisp autumn air whipped around her as she dialed a familiar number. She had a hunch that whatever was brewing in Polkville was bigger than a single exploding gas station, and if anyone had the inside scoop, it would be Sergeant Hawkins.

The line clicked. "Hawkins."

"Sarge, it's Elkins. I'm in Polkville, and things are getting weird out here."

"Weird how?" Hawkins' gruff voice held a note of concern.

Casey quickly filled him in on the details - the attack on Alyson, the explosion at DeRisi's, and the evidence pointing to Tommy Leons' involvement. "Sheriff Ruler thinks there might be a preternatural angle, especially with this tournament coming up. I was hoping you might have some additional intel."

There was a pause on the other end of the line. "Funny you should ask. I've been hearing whispers about an uptick in rei activity in your neck of the woods. Specifically, some chatter about a new player in town, goes by the name of Joseph Bailey."

Casey frowned. The name wasn't familiar. "Bailey? What's his story?"

"From what we've gathered, he's an old-school martial artist. Trained in something called the Way of the Fist. Rumor has it he's got a serious bone to pick with the Yoshimoto clan and their defensive style."

"Yoshimoto? As in Yoshimoto Kwondo?" Casey's mind raced, connecting the dots. "He's the one who trained Sheriff Ruler and his friends, isn't he?"

"Bingo," Hawkins confirmed. "Looks like Bailey's trying to resurrect the old ways. My sources say he's been recruiting disciples, promising to teach them forgotten techniques."

A chill ran down Casey's spine. "Let me guess. Tommy Leons is one of those disciples."

"Got it in one, Elkins. And if Bailey's showing up right before this big tournament, I doubt it's a coincidence."

Casey nodded, even though Hawkins couldn't see her. "So we could be looking at a full-blown rei-fueled martial arts war on our hands."

"It's a possibility. I'll keep digging on my end, see if I can get any more specifics on Bailey's endgame. In the meantime, watch your back out there. If Bailey's as dangerous as the stories suggest, things could escalate quickly."

"Understood, Sarge. I'll keep you posted." Casey hung up, her mind already racing with the implications. If Joseph Bailey was half as ruthless as Hawkins seemed to believe, Alex and his friends could be walking into a deadly trap. She needed to warn them - and fast.

Pocketing her phone, Casey hurried towards her car. She had a sinking feeling that the real battle was just beginning...

****

The old warehouse echoed with the sounds of

combat - the sharp crack of fists against padding, the heavy thud of bodies hitting the mat. Tommy Leons stood at the center of the storm, his chest heaving as he faced off against his mentor.

Joseph Bailey nodded approvingly, circling Tommy with the easy grace of a predator. "You're improving, Leons. Your strikes are harder, more precise. But you're still holding something back."

Tommy narrowed his eyes, sliding back into his stance. "I'm giving it everything I've got, old man. What more do you want?"

"I want you to embrace the true spirit of the Way of the Fist," Bailey said, his voice low and intense. "To not just defeat your opponents, but to destroy them. Body and soul."

Something cold and heavy settled in Tommy's gut. He'd always prided himself on his toughness, his willingness to do whatever it took to come out on top. But the way Bailey talked, it sounded like he was gearing up for a war, not just a tournament.

Bailey must have sensed his hesitation. He stepped closer, his eyes boring into Tommy's. "You want to take down the Marine, don't you? To prove once and for all that you're the top dog in Polkville?"

Tommy nodded, his jaw tight. "More than anything."

"Then you need to be ready to go further than you ever have before. Because I guarantee you, Ruler and his friends won't be pulling their punches." Bailey's hand shot out, faster than a striking snake, and Tommy barely managed to block the blow. "Neither should you."

Tommy's mind flashed back to the explosion at DeRisi's, the smell of gasoline and burnt rubber, the sight of Bobby's lifeless body trapped beneath that car. He'd crossed a line that day, and he knew it. But if it meant finally taking down Alex and cementing his own power, maybe it had been worth it.

He launched himself at Bailey with a renewed fury, his fists and feet lashing out in a relentless barrage. Bailey matched him step for step, his own attacks coming harder and faster. They danced back and forth across the mat, neither giving an inch, until finally Tommy saw an opening. He feinted left, then pivoted right, his elbow slamming into Bailey's ribs with a satisfying crack.

Bailey stumbled back, a flicker of surprise crossing his face before it settled into a grim smile. "There it is. That killer instinct. Nurture that, Leons. Feed it. Because when the time comes, you're going to need every ounce of it."

Tommy nodded, his breath coming in ragged gasps. He could feel the power thrumming through his veins, the dark energy that Bailey had been nurturing in him. It felt good. Dangerous. Like he could take on the whole world and come out on top.

And as he squared up for another round, Tommy silently vowed that when the tournament arrived, he'd do just that. No matter the cost...

****

The old warehouse loomed before Sheriff Alex Ruler and Corporal Larry Armstrong, its rusted walls and shattered windows a testament to years of neglect. But according to their sources, this derelict building had recently become a hub of activity for Tommy Leons and his crew.

Alex glanced at Larry, noting the tension in his friend's shoulders. "Keep your eyes peeled. If Tommy's boys are using this place as a training ground, they're not going to be happy to see us."

Larry nodded, his hand resting lightly on his sidearm. "Roger that, boss. Let's just hope they're in a chatty mood."

They approached the warehouse cautiously, the gravel crunching beneath their boots. As they drew closer, the sound of muffled impacts and grunts of exertion reached their ears. Somebody was definitely putting in work behind those walls.

Alex motioned for Larry to take the side door while he moved towards the front. They took up positions on either side of their respective entrances, weapons drawn. On Alex's silent count of three, they burst inside, ready for anything.

The scene that greeted them was one of controlled chaos. A dozen men, all clad in dark training gear, were spread out across the warehouse floor. Some worked heavy bags, their fists and feet striking with brutal precision. Others sparred in makeshift rings, the clack of wooden training weapons mingling with the smack of flesh on flesh.

But it was the figure overseeing it all that drew Alex's attention. Brutus Bagwell stood at the center of the storm, his massive arms crossed over his barrel chest as he barked orders at the men around him.

"Bagwell!" Alex called out, his voice cutting through the din. "We need to talk."

Brutus turned slowly, his eyes narrowing as he took in the two lawmen. "Well, well. If it isn't Sheriff Ruler and his trusty sidekick. To what do we owe the pleasure?"

Larry bristled at the sidekick comment, but Alex silenced him with a look. "We're investigating a string of incidents that seem to be connected to your boss. DeRisi's murder, the attack on Alyson Jergens. You wouldn't happen to know anything about that, would you?"

Brutus's face was a mask of mock confusion. "DeRisi? Jergens? Sorry, Sheriff, but I've been a little too busy training to keep up with the local gossip."

"Cut the crap, Bagwell," Larry growled. "We know Tommy's up to something. And whatever it is, it's got the whole town on edge."

Brutus chuckled, a deep, menacing sound. "The only thing Tommy's up to is preparing for the tournament. Same as everybody else."

Alex to   ok a step forward, his eyes are hard. "And this 'preparation' wouldn't happen to involve rei energy, would it? Because I've been feeling a lot of that lately. And it's all coming from your direction."

For a moment, something flickered in Brutus's eyes. Fear, maybe. Or anticipation. But it was gone as quickly as it appeared, replaced by a cold, hard smile. "Rei energy? I don't know what you're talking about, Sheriff. We're just a bunch of fighters trying to up our game. Nothing illegal about that."

Alex held his gaze for a long moment, trying to read the truth in those dark, guarded eyes. But Brutus was a stone wall, giving away nothing. Finally, Alex nodded, holstering his weapon. "All right, Bagwell. We'll play it your way for now. But you tell Tommy that I've got my eye on him. And if I find out he's behind any of the weird stuff that's been going on around here, I won't hesitate to bring the full weight of the law down on his head."

Brutus's smile widened, showing far too many teeth. "I'll be sure to pass along the message. Now, if you'll excuse me, I have a training session to get back to."

He turned away, dismissing them with a wave of his hand. Alex and Larry exchanged a frustrated glance, but there was nothing more to be done here. They made their way back out of the warehouse, the sounds of combat echoing behind them.

As they stepped out into the fading sunlight, Larry let out a low whistle. "Well, that was enlightening. Not."

Alex sighed, running a hand through his hair. "Bagwell's covering for Tommy, that much is clear. But there's something else going on here. Something bigger than just the tournament."

"You think it has something to do with this Bailey character Casey mentioned?" Larry asked.

"I'd bet my badge on it," Alex said grimly. "But we can't move on him without proof. We need to keep digging, see if we can find a connection between him and Tommy. Maybe even figure out who is bringing the Relic System into play?"

Larry frowned, his brow furrowing. "The Relic System? You mean those high-tech watches Tommy and his crew have been sporting?"

Alex nodded. "Ken's been doing some digging on them. Turns out they're not just fancy accessories. They're designed to augment the wearer's rei, giving them a massive power boost without the need for traditional training."

"That explains the energy spikes you've been feeling," Larry mused. "But where did Tommy get his hands on tech like that? It's not exactly something you can pick up at the local Best Buy."

"Exactly," Alex said, his mind racing. "And that's where I think Bailey comes in. What if he's the one supplying Tommy with the Relic Systems? Using them to lure in new recruits and rebuild the Way of the Fist?"

Larry's eyes widened. "It's a tempting offer. Get power and skill without all the years of blood, sweat, and tears."

"And if Tommy's any indication, it works," Alex said darkly. "We need to find out more about these Relic

Systems. Where they come from, how they work, and just how widespread their use is."

He pulled out his phone, scrolling through his contacts until he found the one he was looking for. Aidan Kenta. If anyone could uncover the secrets behind the Relic Systems, it would be him.

As the phone rang, Alex felt a flicker of determination amid the growing darkness. They were on the right track, he could feel it. Now they just had to stay one step ahead of Tommy and Bailey.

"Aidan," Alex said as the call connected. "It's Alex. I need your help."

There was a brief pause on the other end of the line. Then, Aidan's voice, calm and measured as always. "What do you need, Sheriff?"

"Everything you can find on the Relic Systems. Design specs, manufacturing details, shipping manifests. I want to know where they come from and who's behind them."

"The Relic Systems?" Aidan sounded intrigued. "I've been curious about those myself. Give me a few hours, and I'll see what I can dig up."

"Thanks, Aidan. But be careful. Something tells me the people behind these things won't take kindly to us poking around."

"Don't worry, Sheriff. Careful is my middle name." With that, Aidan hung up, already typing away in the background.

Alex pocketed his phone, feeling a small weight lift from his shoulders. With Aidan on the case, they were one step closer to unraveling the mystery of the Relic Systems and their connection to Joseph Bailey.

But even as they climbed into Alex's cruiser and pulled away from the warehouse, he couldn't shake the feeling that they were racing against the clock. The tournament loomed on the horizon, and with it, the looming specter of a power that could change the face of Polkville forever.

They needed answers, and they needed them fast. Before the Way of the Fist rose again, and everything they held dear came crashing down...

CHAPTER FIVE

The room was dark, save for the glow of a dozen computer screens casting an eerie blue light across Aidan Kenta's face. He sat hunched over his keyboard, fingers flying across the keys as he delved deeper into the labyrinthine world of Steve Bertinelli's finances.

It had been hours since Alex's call, hours spent combing through shell companies and offshore accounts, searching for the thread that would unravel the billionaire's web of deceit. Aidan's eyes burned from the strain, but he refused to rest. Not when so much was at stake.

He had always known that Bertinelli was a man of secrets, a philanthropist with a shadowy past and a network of connections that stretched from the boardroom to the underworld. But even he had been shocked by the sheer scale of the billionaire's empire. Dummy corporations, money laundering schemes, bribes, and payoffs - it was a maze of corruption that seemed to have no end.

And at the center of it all, a name that kept popping up again and again: Tommy Leons.

Aidan leaned back in his chair, rubbing his tired eyes. The evidence was there, buried deep but undeniable. Bertinelli had been funneling vast sums of money into Polkville for years, much of it going directly to Tommy and his crew. And the timing of the payments lined up perfectly with the appearance of the Relic Systems.

It was the smoking gun they had been looking for, the proof that Bertinelli was the one pulling the strings behind Tommy's rise to power. But it was also just the beginning. Because if Bertinelli was willing to go to such lengths to support Tommy's ambitions, there had to be a reason. A plan that went beyond just winning a tournament.

Aidan's mind raced with possibilities, each more troubling than the last. Was Bertinelli looking to take over Polkville's underworld? To use Tommy and his rei-powered thugs to seize control of the town? Or was there something even bigger at play, a conspiracy that stretched beyond the borders of their little community?

He needed to dig deeper, to follow the money trail wherever it led. But he also knew that time was running out. The tournament was just days away, and if they didn't act soon, it might be too late to stop whatever Bertinelli had planned.

With a renewed sense of urgency, Aidan turned back to his screens, his fingers once again flying across the keys. He had a lead now, a thread to pull. And he wouldn't stop until he had unraveled the whole damn tapestry, no matter where it took him.

In the distance, the first light of dawn was beginning to creep over the horizon, casting a pale glow across the sleeping town of Polkville. But for Aidan Kenta, the real work was just beginning.

****

The steady beep of the heart monitor filled the sterile air of Alyson's hospital room. She lay motionless on the bed, her bruised face a stark contrast to the crisp white sheets. The doctors had assured her that she would make a full recovery, but the physical wounds were only part of the trauma she had endured.

The door creaked open, and Alyson turned her head, wincing at the sudden movement. Her eyes widened as a familiar figure stepped into the room, a duffel bag slung over her shoulder and a look of concern etched on her face.

"Tiffani?" Alyson's voice was hoarse, barely above a whisper.

Her sister rushed to her bedside, dropping the bag and gently taking Alyson's hand in her own. "I came as soon as I heard. Oh, Aly, I'm so sorry. I should have been here sooner."

Alyson shook her head, tears welling in her eyes. "You're here now. That's all that matters."

Tiffani pulled up a chair and sat down, never letting go of her sister's hand. "I spoke to Alex on the way here. He's worried sick about you, Aly. I could hear it in his voice."

Alyson felt a pang of guilt mixed with an old, familiar ache. She and Alex had been high school sweethearts, but she had broken his heart when he left for the Marines. They had eventually found their way back to friendship, but there was still a part of her that wondered what might have been.

"He's a good man," she said softly. "A better friend than I deserve, after everything."

Tiffani squeezed her hand, a knowing look in her eye. "He still cares about you, Aly. Maybe not in the same way as before, but that kind of bond doesn't just go away."

Alyson nodded, pushing away the bittersweet memories. She knew that she and Alex had both moved on, but the echoes of their past still lingered. Shaking off the thought, she focused on the present.

"Tiff, there's something else you should know. Something about Tommy and his crew."

Tiffani frowned, leaning forward. "What is it?"

Alyson took a deep breath, the memories of that awful night flooding back. "They had these devices on their wrists, like high-tech watches. I think they're what's been giving them their powers."

Tiffani's eyes widened. "The Relic Systems," she breathed. "I've been hearing rumors about them, whispers from some of my old contacts in the service. They say they're bad news, Aly. Like, 'end of the world' bad."

Alyson felt a chill run down her spine. If Tiffani was right, then Tommy's rise to power was just the beginning. And if he wasn't stopped soon, the consequences could be catastrophic.

"We have to tell Alex," she said firmly. "He needs to know what he's up against."

Tiffani nodded, already reaching for her phone. "I'll call him right now. And then I'm going to find out everything I can about these Relic Systems. If there's a way to stop them, we'll find it."

As Tiffani dialed Alex's number, Alyson felt a flicker of hope amid the pain and fear. She knew that Alex would stop at nothing to protect Polkville and the people he cared about. And with his team by his side, she believed that they could overcome even the darkest of threats.

Even a monster like Tommy Leons.

****

The old warehouse echoed with the sounds of exertion and pain. Tommy Leons stood at the center of the training floor, his chest heaving and his body slick with sweat. Around him, his men lay groaning on the mats, nursing fresh bruises and bloody noses.

Joseph Bailey circled the group, his eyes cold and appraising. "Again," he barked, his voice cutting through the air like a whip.

Tommy and his crew struggled to their feet, their

faces grim with determination. They had been training non-stop for days, pushing their bodies and their newfound powers to the limit. But Bailey was a relentless taskmaster, always demanding more.

As the men squared off once again, Bailey held up a hand. "Wait," he said, his gaze locking on Tommy. "Leons, step forward."

Tommy obeyed, ignoring the twinge of unease in his gut. He had learned quickly that questioning Bailey was a sure path to pain.

Bailey circled him slowly, his eyes narrowing. "You're holding back," he said, his voice low and dangerous. "You're not embracing the full potential of your rei."

Tommy bristled, his fists clenching. "I'm giving it everything I've got," he growled.

Bailey shook his head. "No, you're not. You're still clinging to the limitations of your physical body. To truly master the Way of the Fist, you must let go of those limitations and become one with your rei."

He held out his hand, and Tommy saw a flicker of energy dance across his palm. "I'm going to teach you a new technique, Leons. One that will help you to unleash the full power of your Relic System."

Tommy's eyes widened, a mix of excitement and trepidation coursing through him. He had seen firsthand the devastating potential of the Relic Systems, but he had never imagined that he could wield that kind of power himself.

Bailey closed his eyes, and the energy in his hand began to pulse and grow. "This technique is called the Cobra Strike," he said, his voice barely above a whisper. "It focuses your rei into a single, devastating point of impact, allowing you to pierce through any defense."

He opened his eyes, and Tommy saw a cold, merciless hunger in their depths. "Watch closely," Bailey said, and then he moved.

It was almost too fast to follow. One moment, Bailey was standing still, his hand wreathed in pulsing energy. The next, he was across the room, his fist buried in the chest of a heavy punching bag. There was a moment of stillness, and then the bag exploded, sand and shredded canvas flying in all directions.

Tommy and his men stared in shock, their jaws slack. Bailey turned back to them, a small, cruel smile playing at the corners of his mouth.

"Your turn, Leons," he said, beckoning Tommy forward.

Tommy stepped up, his heart pounding in his chest. He closed his eyes, reaching out with his senses to the churning well of power within him. He could feel the rei coursing through his body, pulsing in time with his heartbeat.

Slowly, he began to focus that power, channeling it down his arm and into his fist. He could feel it building, growing, until it felt like his entire body was thrumming with barely contained energy.

His eyes snapped open, and he lunged forward, his fist aimed directly at the heart of another punching bag. There was a blinding flash of light, a rush of wind, and then...

Nothing. The bag swayed gently on its chain, completely unscathed.

Tommy stared at it in disbelief, his breath coming in ragged gasps. He had been so sure, so certain that he had tapped into the same power as Bailey. But he had failed.

Behind him, he heard Bailey chuckle softly. "Don't worry, Leons," he said, his voice dripping with false sympathy. "It takes time to master the Cobra Strike. And we have all the time in the world."

Tommy turned to face him, his eyes burning with humiliation and rage. He wanted to lash out, to wipe that smug smile off of Bailey's face. But he knew that he was no match for the older man, not yet.

So instead, he simply nodded, his jaw tight. "I'll keep practicing," he said, his voice low and full of barely contained fury. "I won't stop until I've mastered it."

Bailey's smile widened, and there was a glint of something dark and triumphant in his eyes. "I know you won't," he said softly. "After all, we have a tournament to win, and a Sheriff to destroy."

As Tommy turned back to the punching bag, his mind raced with visions of the future. He saw himself standing over Alex Ruler's broken body, the Cobra Strike crackling in his fist. He saw the look of fear and awe on the faces of the people of Polkville as he claimed his rightful place as their ruler.

And he saw Joseph Bailey standing at his side, a proud mentor and a ruthless ally in the battles to come.

With a growl of determination, Tommy threw himself back into his training, his body and mind focused on a single, consuming goal.

Mastery. Dominance. And the utter destruction of anyone who stood in his way.

****

The Polkville Police Department was unusually quiet, a stark contrast to the bustling chaos that had once filled its halls. In the wake of Sheriff Alex Ruler's dramatic restructuring, the building felt almost ghostly, with only a handful of officers and deputies remaining to carry out the vital work of law enforcement.

In the center of the bullpen, Tai Kwondo and Ken Manson huddled around a large whiteboard, their faces creased with concentration as they pored over the scattered evidence and theories related to the Tommy Leons case. Off to the side, Matt Jones fidgeted in his chair, his youthful energy barely contained as he flipped through a stack of files.

The sound of footsteps echoed through the room, and all three men looked up to see Casey Elkins striding towards them, her expression one of focused determination. She had only recently been granted an office at the Polkville PD, but already her presence had become a vital part of their investigation.

"Gentlemen," Casey said, nodding in greeting as she joined them at the whiteboard. "I hope you've got some good news for me."

Tai sighed, running a hand through his hair. "I wish we did. But the more we dig into Tommy's operation, the more questions we seem to find."

Ken nodded, his brow furrowed. "It's like every lead we uncover just leads to a dead end. We're missing something, but I'll be damned if I know what it is."

Casey studied the board, her eyes narrowing as she took in the web of connections and theories. "What about his associates? Have we been able to track down any of the key players in his organization?"

Matt perked up, waving a file in the air. "I might have something on that front. I've been digging into the backgrounds of some of Tommy's known associates, and I think I found a connection to a larger criminal network."

Casey turned to him, her interest piqued. "Go on."

Matt flipped open the file, pointing to a series of grainy surveillance photos. "See this guy? That's Vince Raymon, one of Tommy's top enforcers. I've been able to track his movements over the past few months, and it looks like he's been making regular trips to Smithfield."

Ken frowned, leaning in for a closer look. "Smithfield? What's in Smithfield?"

"Not much," Matt admitted. "But I did some more digging, and it turns out that there's a shell company based there that's been funneling money into Tommy's operation. A lot of money."

Tai's eyes widened. "How much are we talking?"

Matt swallowed, his face pale. "Millions. And the trail leads back to a name I think we're all familiar with: Steve Bertinelli."

A heavy silence fell over the room as the implications sank in. Steve Bertinelli was a name that had long been associated with organized crime in the area, but he had always managed to stay one step ahead of the law. If he was the one bankrolling Tommy's operation, then they were dealing with a threat far greater than they had ever imagined.

Casey broke the silence, her voice calm and measured. "Okay, this is good. It gives us a place to start. We need to dig deeper into Bertinelli's finances, see if we can find a concrete link between him and Tommy."

Tai nodded, his expression grim. "I'll reach out to Keith and Aidan, see if they can lend a hand with the technical side of things. If there's a digital trail to follow, they'll find it."

Ken cracked his knuckles, a glint of determination in his eyes. "And I'll hit the streets, see if any of my old contacts have heard anything about Bertinelli's movements. If he's up to something, somebody's bound to know about it."

Casey turned to Matt, a small smile playing at the corners of her mouth. "And you, Officer Jones? What's your plan?"

Matt grinned, his enthusiasm infectious. "I'm going to keep digging into Tommy's associates, see if I can uncover any more connections to Bertinelli or his network. If there's a weak link in his chain, I'll find it."

Casey nodded, her smile widening. "Good. Let's get to work."

The sun was just beginning to dip below the horizon as Sheriff Alex Ruler and Corporal Larry Armstrong pulled into the parking lot of the Polkville Police Department. The two men were silent as they exited the vehicle, their faces grim and their bodies tense with the weight of what they had discovered.

As they made their way inside, the usual bustle and energy of the department seemed muted, as if the very walls could sense the gravity of the situation. The few officers and staff members they passed in the halls nodded in greeting, but there was a wary edge to their expressions, a sense of unease that hung heavy in the air.

Alex and Larry headed straight for the conference room, where they knew the rest of their team would be waiting. As they pushed through the doors, they were greeted by a sea of anxious faces: Tai Kwondo, Ken Manson, Matt Jones, and Casey Elkins, all huddled around a large table covered in files and evidence bags.

"What did you find?" Tai asked without preamble,

his voice tight with tension.

Alex sighed, running a hand through his hair. "Nothing good," he said grimly. "We tracked down Brutus Bagwell and some of Tommy's other top men at an old warehouse on the outskirts of town. They were in the middle of some kind of training session, and the energy coming off of them was like nothing I've ever felt before."

Larry nodded, his expression dark. "It was like they were supercharged with rei, like they had tapped into some kind of power source we've never seen before. And the way they were moving, the techniques they were using... it was like they were preparing for war."

Casey leaned forward, her eyes narrowing. "The Relic Systems," she said softly. "It has to be."

Ken frowned, glancing down at the files in front of him. "But where are they getting them from? And why now, right before the tournament?"

"I think I might have an answer to that," Matt said, his voice hesitant. All eyes turned to him as he pulled out a file from the stack in front of him. "I've been digging into Tommy's financials, trying to track down the source of his funding. And I found a connection to a shell company based in Smithfield, one that's been funneling millions of dollars into his operation over the past few months."

Alex's eyes widened. "Smithfield? That's Steve Bertinelli's territory."

Matt nodded, his face pale. "Exactly. And the money

trail leads straight back to him. He's been bankrolling Tommy's operation from the beginning."

A heavy silence fell over the room as the implications sank in. They had always known that Tommy was a dangerous man, a criminal with a lust for power and a ruthless streak a mile wide. But if he had the backing of someone like Steve Bertinelli, a man with vast resources and a network of corruption that stretched across the entire East Coast...

"This is bigger than we thought," Tai said quietly, voicing the thought that was on all of their minds. "If Bertinelli is involved, then we're not just dealing with a small-time thug anymore. We're talking about organized crime on a massive scale."

Casey nodded, her expression grim. "And if they're using the tournament as a cover to distribute the Relic Systems and expand their power base..."

"Then we don't have much time," Alex finished, his voice hard. "We need to find out exactly what they're planning, and we need to stop them before it's too late."

He looked around the room, meeting the eyes of each member of his team in turn. They were a small group, a handful of dedicated officers and specialists up against a criminal empire with seemingly limitless resources. But they were also the best of the best, hand-picked by Alex himself for their skills, their integrity, and their unwavering commitment to justice.

"Alright, people," he said, his voice ringing with authority. "You know what we're up against. You know what's at stake. But I also know that there's nobody else I'd rather have by my side in this fight. We're going to take these bastards down, and we're going to do it together. No matter what it takes."

As the team nodded in agreement, their faces set with determination, Alex felt a flicker of hope amid the gathering darkness. They were up against the odds, facing an enemy that seemed to grow more powerful by the day. But they were also the best hope that Polkville had, the thin blue line that stood between the innocent and the evil that threatened to consume them all.

And with his team by his side, Alex knew that there was no challenge they could not overcome, no darkness they could not face. They would stand together, united in their purpose, and they would not rest until justice was served.

The battle for Polkville's soul had begun, and they would fight to the very end.

CHAPTER SIX

As Alex entered the hospital room, he was struck by a sense of déjà vu. Alyson lay in the bed, her bruises stark against her pale skin, while Tiffani sat beside her, holding her hand. It was a scene that could have been pulled from their high school days, when the three of them had been inseparable.

"Alex," Tiffani said, looking up with a smile. "It's good to see you again."

Alex returned the smile, setting a bouquet of flowers on the bedside table. "You too, Tiff. It's been too long."

Alyson glanced between them, a hint of amusement in her eyes despite the pain she was in. "You two remember each other, then?"

Tiffani laughed, the sound filling the room with warmth. "How could I forget? This is the guy I had to practically shove in your direction back in high school."

Alex ducked his head, a flush creeping up his neck. "Hey, I would have gotten there eventually."

"Sure you would have," Tiffani teased. "Around the same time Aly here figured out how to parallel park."

Alyson swatted at her sister's arm, a grin tugging at her lips. "I wasn't that bad."

"You keep telling yourself that, sis."

For a moment, the years fell away and they were teenagers again, laughing and joking without a care in the world. But then Alex's gaze fell on Alyson's injuries, and reality came crashing back.

He sat down on the edge of the bed, his expression growing serious. "Aly, I'm so sorry this happened to you. If I had known..."

Alyson shook her head, cutting him off. "This isn't your fault, Alex. You couldn't have known what Tommy was capable of."

Tiffani's grip on Alyson's hand tightened, her eyes flashing with anger. "But he's going to pay for it. Right, Alex?"

Alex met her gaze, his jaw set with determination. "You can count on it. My team and I, we're going to bring Tommy Leons and his boss Steve Bertinelli to justice. We won't let them get away with this."

Alyson leaned back against the pillows, her eyes drifting closed. "I know you won't," she murmured. "I trust you, Alex. I always have."

Tiffani   watched her sister for a moment,

then turned back to Alex. "She's been through a lot," she said softly. "More than anyone should have to go through."

Alex nodded, his heart aching for the woman he had once loved. Still loved, if he was being honest with himself. "She's strong," he said. "Stronger than she knows."

"She gets that from our mom," Tiffani said with a small smile. "Stubbornness is a Jergens family trait."

Alex chuckled, the sound easing some of the tension in the room. "Don't I know it."

They sat in comfortable silence for a few minutes, watching over Alyson as she slept. Then Tiffani spoke again, her voice low and serious.

"Alex, I meant what I said. Tommy and Bertinelli, they need to pay for what they've done. Not just to Aly, but to all of Polkville."

Alex met her gaze, his eyes burning with a resolute fire. "They will, Tiff. I promise you that. I won't rest until they're behind bars and Polkville is safe."

Tiffani nodded, satisfied. She knew Alex, knew the depth of his commitment and the strength of his character. If anyone could see this through, it was him.

"Good," she said. "Because I'm not going anywhere. I'm in this fight, too. For Aly, for you, for all of us."

Alex reached out, clasping her hand in his. "I wouldn't have it any other way, Tiff. We're in this together, just like old times."

And as they sat there, hands joined and hearts united, a flicker of hope burned bright. The road ahead was dark and the challenges daunting, but they would face them together.

A family, bound by love and fortified by an unbreakable resolve. And together, they would see justice done and their home made safe once more.

No matter the cost.

****

The air in the warehouse was thick with the smell of sweat and the clank of metal as Tommy Leons and his men trained relentlessly. The tournament was just days away, and they were determined to be in peak form.

Tommy stood at the center of the room, his eyes narrowed as he watched his men spar. They were good, he had to admit. The Relic Systems had given them an edge, enhanced their strength and speed to superhuman levels. But would it be enough?

He thought back to his last conversation with Steve Bertinelli, the man who had bankrolled his entire operation. Bertinelli had been clear: the tournament was their chance to seize control of Polkville, to eliminate the competition and establish their dominance once and for all.

And Tommy had no intention of failing.

He stepped forward, his voice cutting through

the din of the training. "Listen up," he barked. "The tournament is just around the corner. This is what we've been working for, what we've been training for. And I expect nothing less than victory from each and every one of you."

The men stopped their sparring, turning to face their leader. They knew the stakes, knew what was expected of them.

Tommy began to pace, his eyes roving over his assembled fighters. "Sheriff Ruler and his team think they can stop us," he said, his lip curling in a sneer. "They think they can bring us down. But they have no idea what they're up against."

He held up his wrist, the Relic System glinting in the harsh light. "With these, we are unstoppable. We are the future of Polkville, and we will crush anyone who stands in our way."

The men cheered, their voices rising in a cacophony of support. They were ready, eager to prove themselves and claim their place at the top.

Tommy smiled, a cold and cruel thing. "But we can't get complacent," he warned. "Ruler and his deputies are resourceful. They'll be coming at us with everything they've got. So we need to be ready for anything."

He gestured to Brutus and Chris, his two top lieutenants. "Double the patrols around the warehouse," he ordered. "I want eyes on every entrance, every possible point of infiltration. If Ruler and his team breathe in our direction, I want to know about it."

The men nodded, already moving to carry out their orders. Tommy watched them go, a sense of anticipation building in his chest.

This was his moment, his chance to finally seize the power he had always craved. And he would not let it slip through his fingers.

He thought of Alyson Jergens, the woman he had once tried to break. She had been a message, a warning to Sheriff Ruler and anyone else who dared to challenge him.

But she had survived, and now she was a symbol of defiance. A rallying point for those who would stand against him.

Well, he would just have to break her again. Break her, and anyone else who got in his way.

Starting with Alex Ruler.

Tommy's fist clenched, the Relic System pulsing with energy. He could feel the power coursing through him, the strength of his own will made manifest.

And he knew, with a certainty that bordered on madness, that he would not be denied.

The tournament would be his proving ground, his moment of ultimate triumph.

And when the dust settled and the bodies were counted, Tommy Leons would stand alone atop the ruins of the old order.

The future of Polkville, and beyond.

****

The main classroom of Kwondo's School of Martial Arts thrummed with anticipation as Alex Ruler, master of the Tiger Style, gathered his eclectic team. Beside him stood Chase, his nephew and eager student, already showing promise in the powerful, precise strikes of the Tiger.

Tai, the Dragon Style master, exuded calm control, his fluid movements hinting at the explosive power within. Ken, the Ape Style expert, grinned with a wild, unpredictable energy, his agile mind always seeking an advantage.

Larry and Casey, though lacking formal martial arts training, radiated a raw, innate fighting ability. Their mastery of rei allowed them to hold their own against any opponent.

Aidan, the computer whiz, hung back, his fingers flying over his tablet. Though he typically avoided combat, his technological prowess made him an invaluable asset.

And then there was Keith, the master assassin, his stillness belying the lethal precision of his every move.

"Thank you all for being here," Alex began, his voice resonating with authority. "I know I don't have to tell you how important this is. We're not just fighting for a tournament title. We're fighting for the soul of our community."

He paused, his gaze locking with each of his teammates. "Tommy Leons and Steve Bertinelli think they can take over Polkville. They think their Relic Systems make them invincible. But they don't understand the true strength of our styles, our skills, and our bond."

Tai nodded, his serene expression unshakable. "The Dragon Style teaches us to adapt, to turn our opponent's force against them. Tommy's raw power will be his undoing."

Ken chuckled, cracking his knuckles. "And the Ape Style is all about unpredictability. They won't know what hit 'em!"

Alex smiled, turning to Larry and Casey. "Your innate abilities with rei are a wild card they won't expect. Use that to your advantage, keep them off balance."

The two nodded, a fierce light in their eyes.

"Aidan," Alex continued, "you're our eyes and ears. Monitor everything, find us openings and weaknesses."

Aidan saluted, his tablet at the ready.

Finally, Alex turned to Keith. "And you... do what you do best. Strike hard, strike fast, and leave no trace."

Keith inclined his head, a ghost of a smile on his lips.

"Chase," Alex said, his voice softening as he addressed his nephew. "You've come so far in your training, but remember: the Tiger Style is about precision and control. Stay focused, stay centered, and trust your instincts."

Chase straightened, pride and determination etched on his young face. "I won't let you down, Uncle Alex."

Alex clasped his shoulder, his grip firm and reassuring. "I know you won't. None of you will."

He stepped back, his gaze sweeping the room. "Alright, team. Let's train hard, fight smart, and show Tommy and Bertinelli what true strength looks like. Polkville is counting on us."

As the team dispersed, each moving to hone their unique skills, Alex felt a surge of confidence. They were a diverse group, each bringing something special to the table. And together, they were unbeatable.

Tommy Leons and Steve Bertinelli were about to learn a hard lesson: never underestimate the power of a unified team, bound by loyalty, skill, and an unshakeable commitment to justice.

In the Tiger Style, in the Dragon Style, in the Ape Style, and in every style in between, one truth remained constant:

Polkville would not fall. Not on their watch.

The tournament loomed, the enemies gathered, and the stakes couldn't be higher. But Alex and his team were ready.

****

Alyson lay in her hospital bed, her eyes closed but her mind racing. The pain of her injuries had dulled to a constant throb, but the emotional scars ran deep. She felt violated, broken, and above all, angry. Angry at Tommy for what he'd done, and angry at herself for not seeing the danger sooner.

A soft knock at the door pulled her from her thoughts. Expecting Tiffani or perhaps Alex, she called out, "Come in."

But when the door opened, it wasn't a friendly face that greeted her. It was the last person she wanted to see.

Tommy Leons stood in the doorway, a smirk playing on his lips. He was dressed in a doctor's coat, a stethoscope hanging around his neck. In his hand, he held a Kwondo's School Tag.

Alyson's heart raced, panic rising in her throat. She reached for the call button, but Tommy was faster. He closed the distance in two strides, his hand clamping down on her wrist.

"Now, now," he chided, his voice sickly sweet. "Is that any way to greet an old friend?"

Alyson stared at him in disbelief, her fear giving way to fury. "How did you get in here?" she demanded. "Alex said-"

"Alex says a lot of things," Tommy interrupted, his grip tightening. "But he's not as smart as he thinks. All it took was a stolen coat, a fake tag, and a little bit of charm with the nurses. Amazing what people will overlook when you look the part."

He leaned in closer, his breath hot on her face. "But then, you know all about being overlooked, don't you, Alyson? Poor little Alyson, always in the shadow of her sister, her friends, her precious Alex."

Alyson flinched, his words cutting deep. But she refused to let him see her pain. "What do you want, Tommy?" she asked, her voice cold as steel.

Tommy's smile widened, his eyes glinting with malice. "I want you to understand," he said softly. "I want you to understand what happens when people cross me. When they try to stand in the way of what I want."

He released her wrist, his hand drifting to her cheek in a grotesque parody of affection. "You thought what happened at your house was bad? Oh, Alyson. That was just the beginning."

Alyson's blood ran cold. "What are you talking about?"

Tommy's smile turned cruel. "After we left you there, broken and bleeding, I had my boys pay a little visit to your house. A little parting gift, you might say."

He leaned in, his lips brushing her ear. "They burned it to the ground, Alyson. Everything you owned, everything you loved... all gone. Just like that."

Alyson's world spun, the horror of his words sinking in. Her home... her sanctuary... gone. Destroyed by this monster, just as he'd tried to destroy her.

Tears stung her eyes, but she blinked them back, refusing to give him the satisfaction. "You're sick," she whispered. "You're a sick, twisted bastard, and you're going to pay for what you've done."

Tommy laughed, the sound harsh and grating. "Oh, I don't think so," he said. "In fact, I think you're going to keep this little visit just between us."

Alyson stared at him incredulously. "And why would I do that?"

Tommy's smile turned sly. "Because of Alex, of course. Your precious, noble Alex. How do you think he's going to react when he finds out what happened to you? What we did to you?"

He traced a finger down her cheek, his touch making her skin crawl. "Do you really think he could ever look at you the same way? Knowing that you've been touched, tasted, by other men? By me?"

Alyson's heart clenched, her deepest fears laid bare. "He... he loves me," she whispered, but even to her own ears, it sounded weak.

Tommy's grin widened, sensing her doubt. "Does he? Can you be sure? I mean, look at you. Broken. Tainted. Used goods. What man would want that?"

He leaned back, his expression mock sympathetic.

"But if you keep quiet, if you don't tell him about our little... indiscretion... maybe he'll never have to know. Maybe you can still keep his love, even if it's based on a lie."

Alyson's mind reeled, torn between her desire to confide in Alex and her fear of losing him. Tommy's words wormed their way into her heart, feeding on her insecurities.

But then, somewhere deep inside, a flicker of defiance sparked to life. A tiny, unbreakable part of her that knew the truth.

"No," she said softly, then louder, "No. You're wrong. Alex loves me, truly loves me. And that's not something that can be broken or tainted. Not by you, not by anyone."

She met Tommy's gaze, her eyes blazing with a newfound strength. "He will find out the truth. I will tell him. And he will still love me. And we will make you pay for what you've done."

For a moment, Tommy's mask slipped, a flash of anger and uncertainty crossing his face. But it was gone as quickly as it came, replaced by his usual smug veneer.

"We'll see about that," he said, his voice cold. "We'll see how much he loves you when I'm standing over his broken body at the tournament. When I take everything from him, just like I took everything from you."

He straightened, adjusting his stolen coat. "Get well soon, Alyson," he said mockingly. "I want you there to watch it all come crashing down."

And with that, he turned and walked out, leaving Alyson shaking with a tumult of emotions.

But even amidst the fear and the pain, that spark of defiance grew stronger. A resolve born of love and faith in the man she knew Alex to be.

Tommy was wrong. His cruelty, his mind games... they were nothing in the face of true love. And Alyson's love for Alex? Alex's love for her?

That was unbreakable. Unshakeable. And it would be their greatest weapon in the fight to come.

Alyson closed her eyes, picturing Alex's face. Picturing the future they would build together, once Tommy and his evil were nothing but a distant memory.

"I love you," she whispered into the empty room. "And we will win. Together."

It was a vow. A promise. And Alyson intended to keep it.

No matter what.

CHAPTER SEVEN

The sun was high over Polkville's town square, casting dappled shadows through the leaves of the old oak trees. Alex strolled along the sidewalk, his mind preoccupied with thoughts of the tournament, of Tommy, of Alyson and Casey and the tangled web of his own heart.

He was so lost in thought that he almost didn't notice the sudden hush that fell over the square. The chatter of passersby, the laughter of children, the hum of daily life... all of it seemed to fade away, replaced by a heavy, ominous silence.

Alex looked up, his senses suddenly on high alert. And there, standing in the middle of the square, was Brutus Bagwell.

The hulking man was an intimidating sight, his muscular frame barely contained by his black t-shirt and jeans. But it was the aura of menace that surrounded him, the crackling energy of his Psyjicc powers, that sent a chill down Alex's spine.

"Bagwell," Alex called out, his voice calm but laced with steel. "What are you doing here?"

Brutus grinned, a feral, predatory thing. "Just out for a stroll, Sheriff. Thought I'd take in the sights, maybe have a little fun."

His eyes drifted to a young mother and her child, frozen in fear at the edge of the square. The little girl, no more than six, clutched her mother's hand, her wide eyes fixed on Brutus.

Alex stepped forward, placing himself between Brutus and the civilians. "I don't know what game you're playing, Bagwell, but it ends now. Leave these people alone."

Brutus laughed, a harsh, grating sound. "Oh, I don't think so, Sheriff. See, I've been itching for a good fight, and you just happen to be at the top of my list."

He cracked his knuckles, the Psyjicc energy around him flaring brighter. "So what do you say, Ruler? You and me, right here, right now. Let's give these fine folks a show."

Alex's mind raced, weighing his options. He couldn't let Brutus hurt these innocents, but he also couldn't risk a full-scale battle in the middle of town. The collateral damage would be catastrophic.

Just as he was about to speak, a new voice cut through the tension. "How about you pick on someone your own size, Bagwell?"

Alex turned, his heart leaping into his throat. There, striding into the square with her rei gun drawn, was Casey Elkins.

She moved to Alex's side, her eyes never leaving Brutus. "Alex, get these people to safety. I'll handle this thug."

"Casey..." Alex started, but she cut him off with a look.

"Go. I've got this."

Alex hesitated for a split second, then nodded. He turned to the frightened onlookers. "Everyone, please evacuate the area calmly and quickly. My deputy will escort you to safety."

As the civilians began to move, Alex focused on the young mother and her child. He approached them slowly, his hands held out in a calming gesture.

"It's going to be okay," he said softly. "I'm going to get you out of here. Just stay close to me."

The mother nodded, tears streaming down her face. She scooped up her daughter, holding her close as Alex led them away from the square.

Behind him, he could hear the crackle and hiss of rei energy as Casey engaged Brutus. His heart pounded, every instinct screaming at him to turn back, to help her.

But he had a duty to these innocents. He had to trust Casey, trust in her skills and her strength.

It was the longest walk of his life, every step a battle against his own urges. But finally, he reached the safety perimeter, handing the mother and child off to the waiting officers.

He turned, ready to race back to Casey's aid. But before he could take a step, a hand caught his arm.

It was the little girl, her face streaked with tears but her eyes shining with something like awe. "Thank you, Mr. Policeman," she whispered. "You're a hero."

Alex's heart clenched, a lump forming in his throat. He knelt down, meeting the girl's gaze. "No, sweetheart. The real hero is the lady fighting the bad guy. She's the bravest person I know."

The girl nodded solemnly, then threw her arms around Alex's neck in a quick, fierce hug. Then she was gone, her mother leading her away to safety.

Alex stood, his resolve hardened to steel. He turned back to the square, back to where Casey fought for the soul of Polkville.

He had a job to do. And he would not let her fight alone.

Not now. Not ever.

With a deep breath, Alex Ruler, Sheriff and Guardian of Polkville, ran back into the fray.

****

The town square had become an arena, the stage

for a battle that would echo through the ages. Alex Ruler, the Marine, the Tiger of Polkville, stood tall and proud, his rei energy pulsing around him in a verdant aura. Across from him, Brutus Bagwell, the Psyjic Juggernaut, grinned with savage glee, his own power casting a crimson glow.

"I've been waiting for this, Marine," Brutus snarled, his voice dripping with malice. "Ever since our last fight, I've been hungering for a rematch. And this time, I won't hold back."

Alex smirked, sliding into his signature Tiger Stance. "You think I haven't grown since then, Brutus? You have no idea what you're up against."

The last time we fought, I was caught off guard by his psyjic energy, Alex thought, his mind racing as he analyzed his opponent. *But I've trained, I've studied. I know the secrets of his power now. And I have something he doesn't: a reason to fight beyond myself.*

Brutus roared, his psyjic energy exploding outward in a shock wave of crimson fury. Alex leaped high, riding the wind of his rei to soar above the destruction.

He's strong, Alex realized, *stronger than before. But strength alone won't be enough. Not against the Tiger Style.*

"Witness the power of the Fist Style!" Brutus bellowed. "Maximum Damage!"

His fist became a comet of psyjic might, hurtling towards Alex with devastating force. But Alex was ready. With a swift Tiger Claw, he deflected the blow, the clash of energies sending shockwaves rippling through the square.

I can't let this drag on, Alex thought, his eyes darting to the terrified civilians huddled behind cover. *Every second this battle continues, they're in danger. I have to end it, now!*

"Is that all you've got, Brutus?" Alex taunted, his rei flaring brighter. "I thought you wanted a challenge!"

Brutus snarled, veins bulging in his neck as he poured more psyjic energy into his attacks. "Cobra Blitz!"

A storm of crimson fists rained down on Alex, each blow packing the force of a meteor. But Alex weaved and dodged, his Tiger Style making him untouchable. And with each missed punch, he could see Brutus growing more frustrated, more reckless.

That's it, Alex realized. *His psyjic energy is powerful, but unstable. The angrier he gets, the harder it is for him to control. If I can push him over the edge...*

"What's wrong, Brutus?" Alex called, dancing around another salvo of punches. "Getting tired already?"

"SHUT UP!" Brutus roared, his aura pulsing erratically. "I'll kill you, Marine! I'll kill you dead!"

Now! Alex's mind screamed. "Eye of the Tiger!"

His rei exploded outward, a tsunami of emerald energy that slammed into Brutus like the fist of an angry god. Brutus screamed, his psyjic aura shattering under the onslaught. He crashed to the ground, his body smoking and broken.

Alex stood over him, his rei still swirling around him in a protective cyclone. "It's over, Brutus," he said, his voice calm but stern. "Your psyjic energy has consumed you. You've lost."

Brutus coughed, blood spattering his lips. "H-how?" he wheezed. "How could I lose... to someone like you?"

Alex shook his head. "You fought for power, for yourself. But I fight for something greater. For the people I love, the home I swore to protect." He looked up, meeting Casey's eyes across the square. "That's why I'll always be stronger than you."

As the townspeople emerged from hiding, their cheers ringing through the air, Alex let out a breath he hadn't realized he'd been holding. The battle was won. Polkville was safe.

But in his heart, he knew this was only the beginning. Tommy Leons was still out there, plotting his next move. And Alex would be ready for him.

I'll keep training, he vowed silently. *I'll keep growing stronger. For Alyson, for Casey, for everyone in Polkville. I won't let them down. Not ever.*

The Tiger of Polkville had triumphed once more. But the greatest challenges were yet to come. And Alex Ruler would face them head-on, with the strength of his rei and the love in his heart.

Just you wait, Tommy Leons, he thought, a smile curving his lips. *The Tiger is coming for you.*

****

In the heart of the Polkville Police Department, a group of Alex's closest allies huddle around a bank of monitors, their eyes glued to the screens. On the displays, the titanic battle between Alex and Brutus unfolds, captured in stunning detail by Aidan's citywide security cameras.

Tai, his brow furrowed in concentration, leans in closer to the main screen. "Look at Alex's stance," he murmurs, his voice tight with tension. "He's shifted his weight forward, keeping his center of gravity low. That's a classic Tiger Style defensive posture."

Ken nods, his eyes never leaving the screen. "He's anticipating Brutus's attacks, reading his movements. Our boy's come a long way since their last fight."

On the monitor, Brutus unleashes a devastating barrage of psyjic-enhanced punches, his crimson aura flaring with each strike. But Alex weaves and dodges, his rei-infused reflexes making him a blur of emerald light.

Larry whistles low, shaking his head in admiration. "I've never seen Alex move like that before. It's like he's transcended to a whole new level."

Keith, his expression stoic as ever, nods in agreement. "His rei control has improved dramatically. He's channeling it with a precision and power I've rarely seen."

Aidan, his fingers flying over a keyboard as he works to keep the cameras trained on the action, chimes in. "His vitals are holding steady, despite the intensity of the fight. Alex's endurance and focus are truly remarkable."

Back on the screen, Alex lands a devastating Tiger Claw, the spectral energy raking across Brutus's chest. The Psyjic Juggernaut staggers back, his aura flickering.

Tai's eyes widen, a hint of a smile tugging at his lips. "He's found Brutus's weakness. The instability of his psyjic energy. Alex is pushing him, goading him into overexerting his power."

Ken leans forward, his hands clenching into fists. "Come on, Alex," he mutters under his breath. "Finish this."

On the monitor, Brutus roars with rage and frustration, his aura pulsing erratically. He charges forward, all caution thrown to the wind, his fists engulfed in crimson flames.

Larry shakes his head, his expression a mix of worry and anticipation. "He's lost control. Brutus is running on pure anger now. He's dangerous, unpredictable."

But Keith's eyes narrow, a glint of understanding sparking in their depths. "No," he says softly. "He's exactly where Alex wants him."

As if on cue, Alex's voice rings out from the speakers, calm and clear amid the chaos of the battle. "Eye of the Tiger."

A pulse of pure, blinding rei energy erupts from

Alex's form, engulfing Brutus in a tidal wave of emerald power. The Psyjic Juggernaut's scream of agony and defeat is drowned out by the roar of Alex's triumphant technique.

In the sudden silence that follows, the team exchanges glances of relief, pride, and awe.

Tai is the first to speak, his voice hushed with reverence. "He did it. Alex actually did it."

Ken nods, a grin spreading across his face. "Our Tiger has grown some seriously wicked stripes."

Larry leans back in his chair, his eyes shining with respect. "Polkville's got one hell of a guardian, that's for damn sure."

Aidan, his fingers finally still on the keyboard, looks up at the screen where Alex stands tall amid the settling dust, a beacon of strength and hope. "He's not just Polkville's guardian," he says softly. "He's its future."

Keith says nothing, but the slight curve of his lips and the glint in his eye speak volumes. In this moment, watching their friend and leader triumph against all odds, each member of the team feels a swell of pride, of belonging, of unwavering faith.

Together, they will stand with Alex, through every battle, every challenge, every trial that lies ahead. For they know, with a certainty that surpasses mere belief, that the Tiger of Polkville will never stop fighting for what's right.

As the dust settles on the monitor and Alex stands

victorious, the team takes a moment to absorb the magnitude of what they've just witnessed.

Tai, his expression thoughtful, breaks the silence. "You know, with skills like that, Alex could make a real impact in the tournament."

Ken turns to him, raising an eyebrow. "You think he's ready? I mean, don't get me wrong, our boy just put on one hell of a show. But the tournament... that's a whole different beast."

Tai nods, his gaze still fixed on the screen. "I know it's a risk. But think about it. If Alex enters, and wins... it could change everything. It would send a message to Tommy and his goons that Polkville won't be pushed around anymore."

Larry leans forward, his interest piqued. "It's a bold move, no doubt. But Alex has never been one to back down from a challenge, especially when it comes to protecting his home."

Keith, his voice measured but carrying a hint of anticipation, weighs in. "The tournament would also provide an opportunity to gather intel on Tommy's operations. If his top fighters are there, we could learn more about his plans, his resources."

Aidan, ever the pragmatist, chimes in. "It's a high-stakes gamble. If Alex enters and loses, it could demoralize the town, make Tommy seem even more invincible."

Tai sighs, running a hand through his hair. "True.

But if he wins... it could be the turning point we've been waiting for. The spark that ignites Polkville's fighting spirit."

Ken nods slowly, a grin spreading across his face. "Plus, can you imagine the look on Tommy's face when Alex steps into that arena? I'd pay good money to see that."

The team chuckles, the tension in the room easing slightly at the thought.

Larry stands up, his posture radiating determination. "I say we bring it up to Alex. Let him decide. If he's in, then we'll be right there beside him, every step of the way."

Keith nods, a rare smile tugging at his lips. "As we always are."

Tai looks around at his friends, his teammates, his brothers-in-arms. "Then it's settled. When Alex gets back, we'll talk to him about the tournament. And whatever he decides, we'll face it together. As a team. As a family."

The others nod in agreement, their expressions mirroring the resolve and unity in Tai's words.

On the screen, Alex helps a battered but alive Brutus to his feet, a testament to his strength and his mercy. The Tiger of Polkville, unbowed and unbroken.

And in the hearts of his team, a new fire is kindled. A fire of hope, of determination, of unwavering faith in the man they'd follow to the ends of the earth.

The tournament awaits. And come what may, they will be ready.

CHAPTER EIGHT

The abandoned warehouse was a dimly lit, cavernous space, filled with the echoes of past violence and the weight of dark ambitions. Tommy Leons paced restlessly, his eyes fixed on the far wall where a large map of Polkville was pinned, red circles marking key locations. Beside him, Joseph Bailey sat on a stack of crates, his expression a mix of amusement and calculation.

"Arrested," Tommy spat, his voice dripping with disdain. "Brutus got himself arrested by that damned Marine, Ruler."

Joseph chuckled, the sound cold and sharp in the tense air. "Is that so? Well, it's no great loss. Brutus was always more liability than asset, with that unpredictable psyjicc energy of his."

Tommy whirled on him, eyes flashing. "Don't be so quick to dismiss him, old man. Brutus was a heavy hitter, one of my best."

"Was," Joseph emphasized, his gaze level and

unflinching. "Now, he's a problem. One that needs to be dealt with swiftly and permanently."

Tommy's jaw clenched, but he didn't argue. As much as he hated to admit it, Joseph was right. Brutus had become a loose end, a potential weakness that could unravel everything they'd worked for.

"I've got a guy on the inside," Tommy said after a moment, his tone clipped and businesslike. "He'll make sure Brutus never sees the light of day again."

Joseph nodded, a thin smile playing at the corners of his mouth. "Good. One less distraction. Now, we can focus on what really matters."

He stood, moving to stand beside Tommy at the map. "The tournament. It's our chance to finally put an end to Ruler and his band of do-gooders. To show Polkville, and the world, what true power looks like."

Tommy's eyes traced the lines of the map, his mind racing with possibilities. "It's more than that," he said slowly, his voice low and intense. "It's my chance to prove myself to Bertinelli. To show him that I'm the real deal, the fighter he should be backing."

Joseph raised an eyebrow, intrigued. "Bertinelli? The businessman? What's he got to do with this?"

Tommy's smile was a sharp, vicious thing. "Everything. He's the one pulling the strings, the one with the real power. And he's got his eye on some hotshot fighter, Douglas Kincaid. Thinks he's the future of the Way of the Fist."

He turned to face Joseph, his eyes burning with determination. "But he's wrong. I'm the future. And at the tournament, I'm going to prove it. I'm going to crush Kincaid, crush Ruler, crush anyone who gets in my way. And then Bertinelli will see, they'll all see, that Tommy Leons is the name they should fear."

Joseph's hand came to rest on Tommy's shoulder, the grip firm and unyielding. "And they will, my boy. With my training, my guidance, you'll be unstoppable. Ruler, Kincaid, Bertinelli... they won't know what hit them."

In the shadows of the warehouse, the two men stood, their forms cast in stark relief by the single flickering light above. United in purpose, in ruthless ambition, in their hunger for power and control.

But even in this moment of solidarity, the specter of Steve Bertinelli loomed large, an unseen puppetmaster pulling the strings from afar. For in the game they played, power was a fickle mistress, and loyalty, a currency easily bought and sold.

****

Alyson leaned heavily on Alex as he guided her through the door of her apartment, his arm wrapped securely around her waist. Tiffani, Tai, and Ken followed close behind, each laden with boxes and bags containing Alyson's belongings. The space was modest but inviting, a welcome respite after the trials of the past few weeks.

"Easy now, Aly," Alex murmured, his voice soft with concern. "We're home."

Alyson managed a small smile, the fading bruises on her face a stark reminder of all she had endured. Her eyes glistened as she surveyed the familiar surroundings. "Home," she echoed, her voice thick with emotion. "I wasn't sure I'd ever see it again."

Tiffani set her box down and moved to her sister's side, offering a gentle touch of comfort. "You're safe now, Aly. We're all here for you."

Tai and Ken nodded in agreement, their expressions warm and supportive. "Anything you need, Alyson," Tai assured her, "just say the word."

"We've got your back, always," Ken added, his usual grin softening into a look of sincere affection.

Alyson's smile widened, a single tear escaping down her cheek. "I know. I can't thank you all enough, for everything."

Alex carefully helped her to the couch, easing her down onto the cushions. "You never have to thank us, Aly. We're family."

He turned to the others, gratitude mingling with a hint of nervous anticipation in his expression. "Speaking of which, could you guys give us a minute? There's something I need to talk to Alyson about."

The trio exchanged knowing looks, a silent understanding passing between them. "Of course,"

Tiffani replied, her tone gentle. "We'll just unpack a few things in the kitchen."

"Yeah, gotta make sure Alyson's got all her favorite snacks," Tai chimed in, his eyes twinkling.

Ken couldn't resist a playful jab. "And hide the ones Alex likes, so he doesn't eat them all."

Laughter rippled through the group, a welcome respite from the heavy emotions of the moment. As the three friends made their way to the kitchen, Alex settled beside Alyson, his expression growing serious.

"Aly, there's something I need to tell you. About your house."

Alyson   's breath hitched, her eyes widening with a mix of fear and painful remembrance. "Alex, I... I don't know if I can face going back there, after what happened..."

He took her hand in his, his touch a reassuring anchor. "You won't have to. I've arranged for a crew to come out and rebuild, from the ground up. A fresh start, for when you're ready."

Tears welled anew in Alyson's eyes, her gaze locked with his. "Alex, I can't... that's too much, you don't have to..."

"I want to," he interjected gently. "Aly, I... I need you to know something." He paused, taking a deep, steadying breath. "I love you, Alyson. I always have, and a part of me always will. What we had, it was special, and it will always mean the world to me."

The tears spilled over, tracing silent paths down Alyson's cheeks. "I love you too, Alex. I'm so sorry for how things ended between us, for pushing you away..."

Alex shook his head, a sad, understanding smile on his lips. "Don't be sorry, Aly. We were young, we both made mistakes. But that's the past. What matters is now, and the future." He hesitated, gathering his courage. "And in that future, I... I see someone else, standing by my side."

Realization dawned in Alyson's eyes, a flicker of acknowledgment and acceptance. "Casey," she breathed.

He nodded, his expression a mix of tenderness and trepidation. "Yes. Aly, I... I think I'm falling for her. Falling hard. And I need you to know that it doesn't change how much I care about you, how much I'll always be here for you."

Silence stretched between them, weighted with the enormity of the moment. Then, slowly, a smile bloomed on Alyson's face. It was a smile tinged with sadness, but also with genuine warmth and understanding. "Alex... you deserve to be happy. And if Casey makes you happy, then I'm happy for you."

She squeezed his hand, her eyes shining with affection. "You'll always be my best friend, my protector, my... my Alex. And that's enough. More than enough."

Alex pulled her into a tight embrace, his own eyes damp with emotion. "Thank you, Aly. For understanding, for... for being you."

They held each other, the weight of their shared history, their unbreakable bond, enveloping them like a warm, familiar blanket. In that moment, despite all the pain and heartache, all the challenges and uncertainties that lay ahead... they knew that they would always have each other.

A constant, a touchstone, a reminder of what truly mattered.

Family. Friendship. Love.

As they sat there, wrapped in the comfort of their embrace, the soft murmur of voices and the clinking of dishes from the kitchen washed over them. A reminder that, no matter what the future held, they would never face it alone.

For in the end, it was the love and loyalty between them all, the unbreakable bonds of family and friendship, that would see them through the darkest of times and the greatest of challenges.

And with that knowledge, that unshakable faith, they were ready to face whatever came next... together.

As Alex and Alyson sat on the couch, the weight of their shared history and the depth of their bond filling the space between them, Alyson's expression grew thoughtful. She studied Alex's face, taking in the play of emotions in his eyes, the tender curve of his smile.

"Alex," she began, her voice soft but steady, "if Casey is going to be a part of your life, a part of your future... I want to meet her."

Alex blinked, a flicker of surprise crossing his features. "You want to meet Casey?"

Alyson nodded, a determined glint in her eye. "I do. I need to know that she's right for you, that she... that she has good intentions with your heart."

A warm chuckle escaped Alex's lips, his expression a mix of amusement and affection. "Aly, are you planning on giving her the third degree?"

She swatted his arm playfully, a hint of her old spirit resurfacing. "No, you goof. But I do want to talk to her, woman to woman. I want to make sure she understands how special you are, how much you mean to me... to all of us."

Alex's gaze softened, a lump forming in his throat. "Aly..."

"I know you can take care of yourself," she continued, her tone gentle but insistent. "But you've got a big heart, Alex. You give so much of yourself to others, to protecting and helping and being there for everyone. I just... I need to know that Casey sees that, that she appreciates it. That she'll be there for you, the way you've always been there for me."

Tears pricked at the corners of Alex's eyes, his heart swelling with love and gratitude. "I... I don't know what to say, Aly. That means more to me than I can express."

Alyson smiled, reaching up to brush a stray tear from his cheek. "You don't have to say anything, Alex. Just promise me you'll set up a time for me and Casey to talk.

Maybe over coffee, or dinner. Something low-key, where we can really get to know each other."

Alex nodded, covering her hand with his own. "I promise. I'll talk to Casey, see when she's free. I think... I think she'd really like that, getting to know you better."

"I hope so," Alyson replied, a glimmer of mischief in her eye. "Because if she's going to be part of the family, she'd better be ready for the full Alyson Jergens experience."

Laughter bubbled up in Alex's chest, the sound bright and cleansing. "Oh, she has no idea what she's in for."

They grinned at each other, the moment of levity a welcome respite from the heavy emotions of earlier. As their laughter faded, a comfortable silence settled over them, the bond between them stronger than ever.

"Thank you, Aly," Alex said softly, squeezing her hand. "For everything. For being the amazing, caring, protective friend that you are."

Alyson leaned into him, resting her head on his shoulder. "Always, Alex. That's what family does. We look out for each other, no matter what."

They sat like that for a long moment, drawing strength and comfort from each other's presence. And though the future was uncertain, though the challenges ahead loomed large and daunting, they knew that they would face them together.

As a family. As friends. As the unbreakable heart of

Polkville.

In the kitchen, the murmur of voices and the clatter of dishes continued, a soothing backdrop to the quiet moment in the living room. Tiffani, Tai, and Ken moved about their tasks, their presence a constant reminder of the love and support that surrounded Alex and Alyson.

****

The sun had barely crested the horizon when Alex, Tai, Ken, and the rest of their team gathered at Kwondo's School of Martial Arts. The usually bustling space was eerily quiet, the only sound the soft scuff of feet on the polished wooden floor.

Alex stifled a yawn, his eyes still heavy with sleep. "Remind me again why we're here at this ungodly hour?"

Tai, looking far too alert for the early morning, grinned at his friend. "Because, my dear Alex, we have a special guest instructor today. Someone who's going to help us take our training to the next level."

As if on cue, the door to the school slid open, revealing a figure silhouetted against the rising sun. As the person stepped inside, the team's eyes widened in collective surprise.

It was a woman, tall and lean, with a shock of bright red hair pulled back into a tight ponytail. She moved with the grace and precision of a dancer, each step fluid and purposeful. But it was her eyes that truly commanded attention - a piercing, vivid green that seemed to see straight into the soul.

"Everyone," Tai said, his voice ringing with pride, "I'd like you to meet my cousin, Jeet Kun Kwondo."

Jeet bowed deeply, a smile playing at the corners of her mouth. "It's an honor to meet you all. Tai has told me so much about you."

Ken, never one to be fazed for long, stepped forward with a grin. "The honor is ours, Jeet. But I gotta ask - what brings you to our humble little town?"

Jeet's expression grew serious, her gaze sweeping over the assembled team. "I heard about what's been happening here. About the threats you're facing, the battles you're fighting. And I knew I had to come, to help in any way I can."

Alex felt a surge of gratitude, mixed with a twinge of curiosity. "We appreciate that, Jeet. But how exactly do you plan to help?"

The smile returned to Jeet's face, this time with a hint of mischief. "By pushing you to your limits, and then beyond. By showing you what you're truly capable of, when you let go of your doubts and fears and embrace your full potential."

She clapped her hands together, the sound sharp and commanding in the quiet of the school. "So, who's ready to get started?"

What followed was a training session unlike anything the team had ever experienced. Jeet was a masterful instructor, guiding them through a series of exercises and drills that challenged them physically, mentally, and emotionally.

She worked with each member individually, honing their strengths and shoring up their weaknesses. For Alex, she focused on his Tiger Style, pushing him to refine his technique and tap into the full power of his rei.

"Remember, Alex," she said, her voice low and intense as they sparred, "the Tiger is not just about strength. It's about precision, control, and the ability to adapt to any situation. Embrace that flexibility, that fluidity, and you'll be unstoppable."

For Tai, she delved into the intricacies of his Dragon Style, helping him to harness his inner fire and channel it into every strike and block.

"The Dragon is a creature of passion, Tai," she reminded him, her eyes blazing. "Let that passion fuel you, but don't let it consume you. Find the balance between the fire and the calm, and you'll be a force to be reckoned with."

And for Ken, she focused on the unpredictable, acrobatic nature of his Ape Style, encouraging him to lean into his natural agility and creativity.

"The Ape is a trickster, Ken," she grinned, as he executed a particularly complex flip. "Embrace that spirit of playfulness, of spontaneity. Let your opponents think they have you figured out, then surprise them with a move they never saw coming."

As the session wore on, the team's energy and

excitement grew. They could feel themselves getting stronger, faster, more in tune with their own abilities and each other.

During a break, as they gulped down water and mopped the sweat from their brows, Tai broached the subject that had been on everyone's mind.

"Guys," he said, his voice serious but tinged with anticipation, "I think it's time we consider entering the tournament."

Alex and Ken exchanged a glance, a silent conversation passing between them. Finally, Alex nodded, a determined glint in his eye.

"I agree. We've been training hard, getting stronger every day. And with Jeet's help, I think we have a real shot at winning this thing."

Ken grinned, cracking his knuckles. "Plus, can you imagine the look on Tommy's face when we wipe the floor with him and his goons in front of the whole town?"

Tai chuckled, clapping his friends on the shoulder. "Then it's settled. We'll enter as a team - the three of us, representing the best that Polkville has to offer."

Jeet, who had been listening quietly, stepped forward, her expression proud. "I think that's an excellent idea. And I'll be with you every step of the way, helping you prepare and strategize."

She looked at each of them in turn, her gaze fierce and unwavering. "Together, we'll show Tommy Leons and everyone else what true strength, true power, really looks like. We'll show them the heart and soul of Polkville, and why it can never be broken."

The team nodded, their faces set with determination and purpose. They knew the road ahead would be difficult, the challenges daunting. But they also knew that they had each other, and the unbreakable bond of family and friendship that would see them through.

As they returned to their training, their movements sharper, their focus laser-keen, a new sense of hope and excitement filled the air.

CHAPTER NINE

The sun was high in the sky, casting a warm glow over the streets of Polkville as Alex and Casey cruised through town in Alex's 1967 Chevelle. The iconic car, painted a vibrant lime green with a striking amalgam of a Tiger, Ape, and Gorilla emblazoned on the hood, turned heads as it rumbled down the road. The windows were down, the breeze ruffling their hair, and the radio played softly in the background, a nostalgic tune that seemed to capture the essence of the moment.

Casey laughed at something Alex said, her eyes sparkling with mirth and affection. "I still can't believe you actually stole Old Man Johnson's tractor for a joyride," she grinned, shaking her head. "I always knew you were a rebel, but that's next level."

Alex chuckled, his hand finding hers on the seat between them. "Hey, in my defense, I was young and stupid. And it seemed like a good idea at the time."

"Don't they all," Casey teased, intertwining her fingers with his. "But I have to admit, I kind of like the idea of you as a wild child. It's a side of you I haven't seen before."

Alex's smile softened, his thumb tracing gentle circles on the back of her hand. "Well, stick around long enough, and you might just see a few more."

They fell into a comfortable silence, the connection between them palpable and warm. It was a new thing, this growing closeness, but it felt right, natural. Like a puzzle piece sliding into place.

After a few minutes, Alex cleared his throat, a thought occurring to him. "Hey, what do you say we make a little detour? There's someone I'd like you to meet."

Casey raised an eyebrow, intrigued. "Oh? And who might that be?"

"Alyson," Alex replied, his tone gentle but serious. "She's... well, she's important to me. And I think it would mean a lot to her, to meet you. To see the person who's making me so happy."

Casey's expression softened, a flicker of understanding passing over her features. "Alyson... your ex, right? The one who was attacked?"

Alex nodded, a shadow passing over his face at the memory. "Yeah. She's been through a lot, but she's one of the strongest people I know. And she's always been there for me, even when... even when things between us were complicated."

Casey squeezed his hand, a silent show of support. "I'd love to meet her, Alex. If she's important to you, then she's important to me, too."

Alex's heart swelled with gratitude and affection. "Thank you, Casey. That means more to me than you know."

With a quick turn of the wheel, Alex steered the Chevelle towards Alyson's apartment, the powerful engine roaring as they accelerated. The amalgamated beast on the hood seemed to come alive, a reflection of the strength, resilience, and unity that defined Alex and his team.

The knock on the door was soft but insistent, pulling Alyson from her thoughts as she sat curled on the couch, a steaming mug of tea cradled in her hands. Tiffani, who had been puttering around the kitchen, wiping down counters and putting away dishes, paused in her work, her brow furrowing.

"You expecting someone, Aly?" she asked, already moving towards the door.

Alyson shook her head, setting her mug down on the coffee table. "No, not that I can think of."

Tiffani shrugged, peering through the peephole. Her eyes widened, a grin spreading across her face as she quickly undid the locks and pulled the door open.

"Alex!" she exclaimed, stepping aside to let him enter. "And you must be Casey. We've heard so much about you."

Casey smiled, extending her hand. "All good things, I hope. It's wonderful to finally meet you, Tiffani."

As the two women shook hands, Alex stepped into the apartment, his eyes immediately finding Alyson's. A silent conversation seemed to pass between them, a mix of warmth, understanding, and a hint of nervousness.

"Aly," Alex said softly, moving to her side. "I hope it's okay that we dropped by. There's someone I really want you to meet."

Alyson's gaze shifted to Casey, taking in the other woman's kind eyes and easy smile. Slowly, she stood, smoothing down her shirt with slightly trembling hands.

"Of course it's okay," she said, her voice steady despite the fluttering in her chest. "I've been looking forward to this."

She stepped forward, holding out her hand to Casey. "It's nice to meet you, Casey. I'm Alyson."

Casey took her hand, her grip warm and firm. "The pleasure is mine, Alyson. Alex has told me so much about you. I feel like I know you already."

Alyson's smile grew a touch more genuine, the sincerity in Casey's voice putting her at ease. "Well, I hope I can live up to the hype."

They all laughed, the tension in the room dissipating like mist in the sun. Tiffani, ever the gracious host, ushered them all to the couch, insisting on getting drinks and snacks.

As they settled in, the conversation began to flow, easy and natural. Casey asked about Alyson's recovery, her work at the diner, her hopes and dreams for the future. Alyson, in turn, inquired about Casey's job with the RIPD, her experiences in Polkville, and how she and Alex had first met.

Through it all, Alex sat back, a contented smile on his face as he watched two of the most important women in his life connect and bond. There was no jealousy, no awkwardness, just a sense of rightness, of pieces falling into place.

Alyson leaned forward, her expression growing serious. "Casey, there's something you should know about Jordan Reyes. Something that not many people are aware of."

Casey tilted her head, curiosity piqued. "What is it?"

Alyson took a deep breath, steeling herself. "Reyes wasn't just the former Sheriff. He was also in league with Tommy Leons."

Casey's eyes widened, shock registering on her face. "What? How do you know this?"

Alyson's hands clenched into fists, painful memories resurfacing. "I overheard them talking, once. It was right before Alex came back to town. Reyes and Leons, they were discussing some kind of deal, something about Reyes turning a blind eye to Leons' activities in exchange for a cut of the profits."

She shook her head, disgust and anger mingling in her expression. "I didn't want to believe it, at first. I mean,

Reyes was the Sheriff, he was supposed to protect us. But the more I saw, the more I heard... it all started to add up."

Casey reached out, placing a comforting hand on Alyson's arm. "Alyson, I... I had no idea. This changes everything."

Alyson met her gaze, a fierce determination burning in her eyes. "Casey, if Reyes was working with Leons, there's no telling how deep the corruption in Polkville goes. What if Leons has other people in positions of power, too? What if this is all part of some larger plan?"

Casey's mind raced, piecing together the fragments of information, the nagging inconsistencies that had plagued her since arriving in Polkville. Slowly, a picture began to form, a web of deceit and manipulation that had been strangling the town for who knows how long.

Alyson leaned back on the couch, her expression thoughtful. "You know, it's funny how things work out sometimes. If Alex hadn't become Sheriff when he did, if he hadn't cleaned house the way he did... who knows what would have happened to Polkville."

Casey nodded, understanding dawning on her face. "That's right, Alex fired all the officers that Reyes had hired, didn't he? I remember him mentioning how he wanted to start fresh, build a department he could trust."

Alyson's smile was tinged with pride. "He knew, even then, that something wasn't right. That Reyes and his people were corrupt, that they were more interested in lining their own pockets than protecting and serving the town."

She shook her head, memories of a darker time flickering in her eyes. "It wasn't easy, what Alex did. Firing all those officers, starting over from scratch. But he knew it was necessary, if Polkville was ever going to have a chance at a better future."

Casey reached out, placing a comforting hand on Alyson's arm. "He's a good man, Alex. A brave man. Not many people would have had the courage to do what he did, to take on a system that was so deeply entrenched."

Alyson's smile widened, warmth and affection radiating from her gaze. "That's Alex. Always fighting for what's right, no matter the cost. Always putting others before himself."

She fixed Casey with a meaningful look. "That's why I'm so glad he has you, Casey. Someone who understands him, who shares his values and his dedication. Someone who'll stand by his side, no matter what comes."

Casey felt a lump form in her throat, emotion welling up at the sincerity in Alyson's words. "I... I don't know what to say, Alyson. Except... thank you. Thank you for trusting me, for welcoming me into this family."

Alyson reached out, clasping Casey's hand in her own. "You're one of us now, Casey. And we look out for our own, always."

The two women sat in comfortable silence for a moment, the bond between them stronger than ever. Then, Alyson spoke again, her voice filled with determination.

"You know, just because Alex got rid of Reyes and his corrupt officers... it doesn't mean the fight is over. Leons is still out there, and who knows how many others like him. People who think they can take what they want, hurt who they want, and get away with it."

Casey nodded, her own resolve hardening. "You're right. The battle's not won, not by a long shot. But with Alex leading the charge, with all of us standing together... I know we can make a difference. I know we can make Polkville a safer, better place."

Alyson smiled, a fire burning in her eyes. "Together," she agreed. "Always together."

As the afternoon wore on and the laughter and stories continued to flow, Alyson found herself studying Casey, taking in the warmth of her smile, the intelligence in her eyes, the easy way she leaned into Alex's side.

And in that moment, she knew, with a certainty that filled her heart, that this was the woman meant for Alex. The one who would stand by his side, support him, love him, in all the ways he deserved.

The realization brought with it a sense of peace, of acceptance. Yes, a part of her would always love Alex, always cherish what they had shared. But that love had changed, evolved into something new, something just as precious.

A love built on friendship, on shared history and

unbreakable bonds. A love that wanted, above all else, for Alex to be happy.

And looking at him now, seeing the joy and contentment radiating from every pore, Alyson knew that he was. Happy, and whole, and exactly where he was meant to be.

With Casey, and with the family they had all built together.

As the sun began to dip towards the horizon and Alex and Casey reluctantly prepared to take their leave, Alyson pulled Casey into a warm hug, whispering a heartfelt thank you in her ear.

For making Alex smile again. For being the partner he needed, the love he deserved.

For being a part of this crazy, wonderful, unbreakable family.

Casey hugged her back, understanding passing between them like an electric current. A bond forged in shared love, shared purpose.

And as Alex and Casey walked out the door, hand in hand, Alyson and Tiffani watched them go, matching smiles on their faces.

The future was uncertain, the challenges ahead daunting. But in that moment, none of it mattered.

Because they had each other. And that was enough.

More than enough.

****

The holding cells of the Polkville Police Station were quiet, the silence broken only by the occasional drip of a leaky faucet and the distant hum of the fluorescent lights. In the far cell, Brutus Bagwell lay on a narrow cot, his bruised and battered face turned towards the wall, his mind lost in a haze of pain and regret.

The sound of footsteps echoed down the corridor, jolting Brutus from his reverie. He sat up, wincing as his injured ribs protested the movement. His eyes narrowed as a familiar figure stepped into view.

Tommy Leons stood outside the cell, his expensive suit and polished shoes a jarring contrast to the dingy surroundings. But it was the look on his face that sent a chill down Brutus's spine. Gone was the usual smirk, the air of amused disdain. In its place was a cold, hard fury, a rage that seemed to radiate from every pore.

"You stupid, stupid bastard," Tommy hissed, his voice low and venomous. "Do you have any idea what you've done?"

Brutus flinched, his heart hammering in his chest. He'd seen Tommy angry before, but never like this. Never with this kind of icy, controlled wrath.

"I... I was just trying to take out Ruler," Brutus stammered, his voice hoarse and weak. "I thought if I could beat him, it would send a message, show everyone that we're still in charge..."

Tommy slammed his fist against the bars, the sudden clang making Brutus jump. "You thought? You thought? That's the problem, Brutus. You don't think. You just act, without any regard for the consequences."

He leaned in closer, his eyes boring into Brutus's. "Do you know what the consequences are now, Brutus? Do you know what happens when you get caught, when you end up in a place like this?"

Brutus swallowed hard, a sinking feeling in the pit of his stomach. "I... I won't talk, Leons. I swear. I'll keep my mouth shut, take the fall if I have to..."

Tommy laughed, the sound harsh and mirthless. "Oh, I know you won't talk, Brutus. Because you're not going to get the chance."

He reached into his pocket, pulling out a small, unmarked envelope. He tossed it through the bars, letting it land on the cot beside Brutus.

"That's your ticket out of here, Brutus. A little something to ensure your eternal silence."

Brutus picked up the envelope with shaking hands, a sense of dread washing over him. He opened it, tipping the contents into his palm.

A single pill, small and innocuous, lay in his hand.

He looked up at Tommy, his eyes wide with fear and understanding. "Leons, I... I can't..."

Tommy's face was a mask of stone. "You can, and you will. Because the alternative... well, let's just say it won't be quick. And it definitely won't be painless."

He stepped back from the bars, straightening his suit jacket with a sharp tug. "You've served your purpose, Brutus. But now, you're a liability. And I can't afford liabilities. Not now, not with so much at stake."

Brutus stared at the pill, his mind reeling. This was it, then. The end of the line. The price of his failure, his recklessness.

He closed his fist around the pill, feeling it dig into his palm. A tiny thing, to hold such power over his fate.

"It's been a pleasure, Brutus," Tommy said, his voice dripping with false sincerity. "But all good things must come to an end. And your end... well, it's been a long time coming."

With that, he turned and walked away, his footsteps fading into the distance.

Brutus sat in silence, the weight of his choice bearing down on him like a physical force. Death by his own hand, or a fate worse than death at the hands of Tommy's goons.

In the end, it wasn't much of a choice at all.

Brutus stared at the pill in his hand, his mind racing. Tommy's words echoed in his ears, a death sentence wrapped in a veneer of false sympathy.

He looked up, meeting Tommy's cold, implacable gaze. In that moment, he made a decision.

With a shaking hand, he raised the pill to his lips, making a show of placing it on his tongue. He closed his mouth, holding the pill between his cheek and his teeth, careful not to swallow.

Tommy nodded, a satisfied smirk spreading across his face. "Good man, Brutus. I knew you'd make the right choice."

He turned and walked away, his footsteps fading into the distance.

Brutus waited until he was sure Tommy was gone, then spat the pill out into his hand. He stared at it, a tiny, innocuous thing that had almost been his undoing.

He clenched his fist around it, a grim determination taking hold. Tommy thought he could dispose of him so easily, like a used-up tool to be discarded.

But Brutus wasn't done yet. Not by a long shot.

He had information, knowledge that could bring Tommy's whole operation crashing down. And he knew just the person to share it with.

The one man in Polkville who had a chance of stopping Tommy once and for all.

Sheriff Alex Ruler.

****

Brutus sat at the metal table, his hands cuffed in front of him. The bruises on his face had faded to a mottled yellow, but the determination in his eyes burned brighter than ever.

Across from him sat Alex Ruler, his expression a mix of wariness and curiosity.

"Alright, Bagwell," Alex said, leaning forward. "You said you had something important to tell me. Something about Tommy Leons."

Brutus nodded, a grim smile tugging at his lips. "That's right, Sheriff. Something that could blow this whole case wide open."

He reached into his pocket, pulling out the small, unmarked pill. He placed it on the table between them.

"Last night, Tommy Leons came to my cell. Gave me this. Said it was my 'ticket out of here.' A way to ensure my 'eternal silence,' if you catch my drift."

Alex's eyes widened, realization dawning. "He wanted you to kill yourself. To prevent you from talking."

Brutus chuckled, a harsh, bitter sound. "Got it in one, Sheriff. Tommy's running scared. He knows I've got dirt on him, on his whole operation. And he'll do anything to keep that dirt buried."

He leaned forward, his voice dropping to a conspiratorial whisper. "But here's the thing, Sheriff. I didn't take the pill. I played along, made Tommy think I was going to off myself like a good little soldier. But I've got other plans."

Alex sat back, his mind racing with the implications. "What kind of plans, Brutus?"

Brutus grinned, a fierce, determined light in his eyes. "The kind that'll put Tommy Leons and his whole crew behind bars for the rest of their miserable lives. The kind that'll make this town safe again, for good people like Alyson and your sister."

He tapped the pill with a finger, his gaze never leaving Alex's. "This is just the beginning, Sheriff. The tip of the iceberg. I've got names, dates, locations. Everything you need to bring Tommy down."

Alex stared at him, hope and suspicion warring in his heart. Could this be it? The break they'd been waiting for?

"Why?" he asked finally, his voice quiet but intense. "Why turn on Tommy now, after all this time?"

Brutus sighed, a heavy, weary sound. "Because I'm tired, Sheriff. Tired of the lies, the violence, the constant looking over my shoulder. Tired of being a pawn in Tommy's sick games."

He met Alex's gaze, a flicker of vulnerability in his eyes. "And because... because I want to make things right. I want to do something good, for once in my miserable life."

Alex nodded slowly, understanding dawning. He reached across the table, placing a hand on Brutus's cuffed wrists.

"Alright, Brutus," he said, his voice firm but not unkind. "Let's hear what you've got. And if it's as good as you say... then maybe, just maybe, we can start making things right. Together."

Brutus   smiled, a genuine, grateful smile. For the first time in a long time, he felt a glimmer of hope.

Hope for redemption. For a second chance.

For a future free from the shadows of his past.

CHAPTER TEN

The air crackled with energy as Alex and Tai circled each other on the mat, eyes locked in determination. Tai struck first, a blazing dragon fire trail following his spinning heel kick. But Alex was ready, his ethereal tiger claws flashing as he parried the blow.

"Good read, but watch your footwork!" called Jeet from the sidelines. The two young fighters reset, Tai adjusting his stance at their master's advice.

Alex pressed the attack, a flurry of jabs and claw swipes driving Tai back. But the dragon stylist kept his cool, deftly evading until catching Alex's wrist. With a burst of displacement, they rematerialized across the mat, positions reversed.

"Nicely done displacing," Jeet nodded. "But Alex, you left that opening by overextending."

As the back-and-forth continued, Jeet's sharp eyes missed nothing. A tilt of the hips here, a slight hesitation there - she afforded no blind spots to her elite students.

Finally, she called for a pause, striding onto the mat.

"Tai, come here. There is an ancient Dragon technique called the Dragon Fang OverFang that I will show you..."

Jeet spent several intense minutes guiding Tai through the esoteric forms and opposing energy flows required to master the Dragon Fang OverFang. Pushing and pulling his chi, she commanded him to feel the duality, the push-pull of cosmic forces.

When he finally grasped the intricacies of the Dragon Fang OverFang, a draconian aura engulfed the young man, his rei spiking with untamed power.

"Good, you've accessed its potential!" Jeet nodded approvingly. "Now, put the Dragon Fang OverFang to use! Alex, come at us again with everything you have!"

The training resumed with Tai centered and focus, his newfound skills from the Dragon Fang OverFang allowing him to counter and redirect Alex's searing tiger claw strikes. Where before he had to evade or displace, now Tai could meet Alex's ferocious attacks head-on.

The two fighters traded blows, rei clashing against rei in a dazzling display of martial arts mastery. Even as Alex's tiger claws raked against his defenses, Tai kept his mind clear, employing the duality of the Dragon Fang OverFang to redirect his opponent's ferocious strikes.

"Excellent form!" Jeet called out, her experienced eyes missing nothing. "But don't let your OverFang become a crutch. There is always another way."

Nodding, Tai refocused and rather than deflecting Alex's next attack, he fazed out of corporeality entirely. Blinking back into existence behind his sparring partner, Tai lashed out with a precise dragon fire kick only to find Alex's glowing tiger eyes locked onto him.

"Your displacement won't save you!" Alex roared, his Eye of the Tiger ability allowing him to track Tai's movements. Twin arcs of etherial energy slashed out, catching Tai across the chest with enough concussive force to send him skidding back.

Tai grimaced, batting away the lingering strands of Alex's assault. In that moment, Jeet struck - her movement a blur as she launched herself into their fray.

"A true master is always prepared for more than one opponent!"

Trading blows with her elite students, Jeet's instructions came blazing fast.

"Tai, feel the yin/yang energies, but don't get locked into their cycle!"

An overhead dragon fire slam narrowly missed the diminutive master.

"Alex, push past your limits! Unleash your tiger spirit fully!"

Jeet danced between their furious exchanges, at once encouraging and shutting down their efforts with precise counters. Under her wife tutelage, Alex and Tai found new levels of focus and skill emerging...

Jeet danced amidst the storm of clashing rei energies, her small frame almost supernaturally elusive as she guided her students' growth. Even as Alex unleashed his full tiger spirit fury and Tai melded the yin/yang rhythms of the Dragon Fang OverFang, their combined onslaught could not seem to breach their master's defenses.

"You've learned much," Jeet said, deftly parrying a flurry of blows, "but true mastery comes from synthesizing multiple disciplines!"

On her next evasive backbend, Jeet's movements took on a distinctly different quality. What was once refined Kwondo technique shifted into something more languid yet incredibly precise. Her footwork became light, almost delicate as she transitioned deep into the Crane Style stance.

"The Crane's grace and precision balances the Tiger and the Dragon," she intoned, springing up into a dizzying circuit of flowing hand strikes. "Only by embodying various arts can one triumph over all challenges!"

Alex attempted to close the distance, his claws leading the way, but Jeet's speed was almost blinding. Feinting low, she launched herself in a soaring leap, clearing his guard entirely to rap him twice - once on the crown and again at the base of his skull with two powerseal crane finger strikes.

Tai fared no better, his draconian energies dispersing harmlessly around Jeet's enigmatic zephyr-like movements. A final front snap kick sent the young dragon stylist skidding away to recover his wits.

"The path ahead will not be easy," Jeet stated, resuming her ready stance between them. "But with diligence and the willingness to encompass all that the martial ways offer...victory can be grasped."

Her students could only gaze at their master with newfound awe and determination. If ferocious Tiger and dynamic Dragon were to overcome the obstacles ahead, they would need to emulate Jeet's principle of adaptation and well-rounded mastery.

The training intensified further...

****

The cavernous training room echoed with the sounds of combat - grunts of exertion, impacts against heavy bags, and Tommy's barked commands cutting through it all. His dark eyes missed nothing as he paced around the matted area, the Relic System on his wrist pulsing with baleful energy.

"Again!" he snarled at a sweat-soaked fighter. "Power comes from your base. Root yourself and strike like you mean it to kill!"

Nearby, Joseph Bailey ran another group through an extended demonstration of the Way of the Fist principles. His movements were at once beautiful and terrifying to behold - a synthesis of various disciplines unified into something potent and utterly deadly in his hands. Each strike, each shift of momentum contained the potential for devastation.

"The fist is an honesty few can comprehend," he intoned, delivering a punch that cracked the air itself. "It reveals the true self, separating those who only imagine their path from those who wield it as existence itself."

The other combatants watched raptly, knowing this man's reputation for violence was well-earned. Chris, Vince, Mika, and the rest of Tommy's inner circle struggled to capture even a fraction of Joseph's economy of motion in their own practiced repetitions.

"He makes it look so simple," Vince muttered through gritted teeth, sweat stinging his eyes.

"That's because to a master, it is," a voice replied. Tommy had drifted over, his gaze coolly assessing them all. "Which is why you need to push beyond your limits every second here. Fail, and you're worse than dead to me."

A tense silence fell, driven home by the low thrum of the Relic System. They all knew too well that Tommy's cruelty was matched only by the archaic power contained in that deceptively innocuous bangle, Joseph's teaching paused as Tommy stepped forward, the Relic System's ominous thrum causing the others to tense.

"Enough prattling about your 'true path' nonsense," Tommy said dismissively. "My team doesn't need philosophies. They need results."

Joseph regarded him coolly. "Belief runs deeper than philosophy. You've seen what can be achieved when the flesh embraces the essence of the Way."

"I've seen party tricks," Tommy scoffed. "While you all play at being warriors, I've walked the real path."

His gaze fell onto Chris and Vince, who cowered despite themselves. "You boys need to decide what you're willing to sacrifice. Take Dean here - he grasped that doing what needs to be done separates the weak from the essential."

Chris swallowed hard but met Tommy's stare. "You...you're referring to Brutus? I put him down like you ordered."

"No, you just pulled the trigger," Tommy corrected harshly. "I'm the one who ripped out his ribcage with my bare hands and crushed his trembling heart. I could hear his puppy-like whimpers as the life left that sniveling traitor."

A horrified silence fell over the room. Even Joseph's mask slipped at the graphic retelling. Tommy smiled thinly.

"That's the level of commitment required from all of you. Anything less and you'll end up like poor Brutus - just another obsolete casualty."

Vince couldn't stop his eyes from flickering to the Relic System, its energies seeming to flare brighter at Tommy's words.

"The relics are power...but they're not the only path," Joseph said carefully. "My teachings could help you harness your inner potential without them."

Tommy barked a harsh laugh. "Save your breath. I'll take advantage of every weapon at my disposal, no matter how insignificant it makes you feel. Anyone not willing to do the same is already dead weight."

Pinning the room with a menacing glare, he tapped the Relic System meaningfully.

"This is the new way forward. Get on board or get buried..."

****

The air seemed to crackle with barely contained energy as Jeet danced between Alex and Tai's furious volleys. Her graceful Crane Style technique was a stark contrast to their more aggressive Tiger and Dragon approaches, but a well-timed flurry of strikes from both young fighters still found their marks.

Jeet absorbed the blows with barely a wince, countering with a blindingly fast hand combination that left her students scrambling. "You'll need to do better than—"

The training room doors burst open, interrupting her critique. Casey and the others spilled in eagerly, Keith the assassin immediately moving to join the fray.

"Brought some new targets for you two hot-heads!" Casey called with a laugh, her rei aura already glowing.

Tai had only a beat to react before Ken was on

him, the Ape Style master's technique a dizzying flurry of unpredictable strikes and feints. Nearby, the lumbering Larry met Alex head on, his immense bulk allowing him to shrug off the Tiger Claw slashes.

"I'm not so easy to knock around, cat-boy!" The large man bellowed good-naturedly.

Aidan hung back wisely, taking in the rapidly escalating sparring situation with an eager grin. His eye caught Jeet's knowing look and he could only shrug.

"What? You didn't really think we'd let these two have all the fun, did you Master Jeet?"

The elder martial artist chuckled, settling back into a ready stance as her prized students engaged from multiple fronts now. "Then let's see what you've all got! The path to victory allows for infinite possibilities!"

Chaos erupted within the training room as fists, feet, and rei techniques collided. Under Jeet's watchful guidance, Alex and Tai flowed between battling their friends while still making every exchange a masterful learning experience...

The chaotic sparring match raged on, but Jeet remained an island of calm amidst the whirlwind of strikes and counters. Even as Ken and Larry doubled their efforts against Alex and Tai, the diminutive master deflected their techniques with enviable poise.

"You're all fighting with passion, but passion untamed is just blunt force," she admonished. "Watch and learn..."

In a blur, Jeet was behind Ken, eliminating the Ape Style master's defenses with a rapid-fire combo that left him sprawling. She didn't even pause before sweeping Larry's feet from under him with almost disdainful ease.

"Whoa, Master Jeet's amazing!" Aidan couldn't help but blurt out from the sidelines.

Casey shot him a cocky grin. "Then let's see how she handles this!"

With a determined yell, the young fighter charged in - her rei aura blazing brightly as she opened with a furious volley of strikes and kicks. To Aidan's surprise, Jeet was actually pushed back a step before deftly pivoting to trade blows.

"She's really letting it rip!" he murmured, wrist computer already scanning Casey's kinetic output and energy signatures.

The two fighters moved with almost blinding speed, exchanging rush attacks and counterstrikes that threatened to overwhelm each other. For a moment, it seemed like the younger woman's onslaught might carry the day.

Then Jeet shifted fully into her Crane Style, movements becoming almost aerobic. Hands whipped out to parry the incoming volley before snapping back into position seamlessly.

"Impossible..." Casey panted even as she refused to let up.

With a final twisting evasion, Jeet flowed into Casey's guard to grip her wrist and decelerate her momentum with uncanny gentleness.

"Your flames burn bright, but they lack the tempering of experience," the master said with a kind smile. "Keep stoking that passion and honing your technique, and you may yet surprise me!"

As Casey caught her breath, Aidan was already reviewing the collected data with an awed grin.

Casey struggled to steady her breathing after Jeet had so deftly halted her furious offensive. The young fighter's rei reserves were rapidly draining from her all-out assault against the master's impregnable defenses.

"Your passion burns bright," Jeet repeated with a sage nod, "but your control is still lacking. You must learn to—"

With almost no forethought, Casey's body seemed to move on its own. Drawing what little rei energy she had remaining, the fiery aura around her right fist coalesced into an ultra-dense sphere of flickering power. Then, with a primal yell, she let the concentrated bolt loose straight at Jeet's chest!

The rei bullet crossed the scant distance between

them in a blink. There was no time for evasion or traditional counter-technique. Jeet's eyes went wide as the projectile's leading edge crackled against her crossed guard...

Then it detonated in a searing eruption of unleashed potential!

The shock wave slammed into Jeet with explosive force, blasting her off her feet to crash backwards in a heap. The entire room fell ominously silent, all eyes locked on the dissipating tendrils of Casey's devastating burst.

"Crap, I...I didn't mean to..." Casey gasped, horrified at her own instinctive actions.

But then a low chuckle sounded from the slight crater. With almost unsettling nonchalance, Jeet rose back into a ready stance, lightly brushing off char marks from her smoldering clothes.

"Well now..." she grinned with a look of intense approval. "It seems you have a few surprise techniques left to show me after all!"

Aidan could only gape, his wrist computer fritzing from the overload of data it tried to process from Casey's pointblank detonation.

"Unreal..." he muttered under his breath in awe.

As the shock slowly faded, Jeet's posture somehow made it clear - the true test had only just begun! She beckoned her students to make their next moves.

The air still crackled with residual energy as Aidan's computer frantically ran diagnostics in the wake of Casey's explosive outburst. Warning indicators flashed across the display before stabilizing, allowing the young tech wiz to dig into the compiled data.

"Whoa...Cay, do you have any idea what you just did?" Aidan muttered, eyes widening behind his glasses.

On the training floor, Casey was still catching her breath - almost as stunned as Jeet by the instinctive release of power. The master watched with an appraising eye as Aidan analyzed the readings.

"It seems our friend has stumbled upon an extremely rare manifestation of rei abilities," Jeet stated. "One that separates her from even the most skilled conventional users."

Aidan's fingers danced across the holographic interface, bringing up a high-density energetic diagram that made his eyes go wide. "She's not just guiding ambient rei forces...Casey's rei matrix allows her to directly convert her body's kinetic and thermal energy into volatile dimensional phenomena!"

The others could only blink at the technical jargon, but Jeet nodded sagely. "In layman's terms - her rei bullets do not simply sculpt and project existing power sources. Rather, Casey metabolizes her very movement and fury into localized distortions in reality itself."

"Imbuing each strike with symbiotic potential to detonate pent-up energies," Aidan continued, his tone one of wondering reverence. "It's like her body's constantly on the verge of quantum uncertainty...no wonder the computer almost crashed trying to model it!"

All eyes turned towards the young woman, who could only offer a sheepish shrug. Casey may not have fully grasped the science behind it, but the dawning looks of respect from her friends and master spoke volumes.

"Rei mastery comes in innumerable flavors," Jeet concluded. "But that sort of wild, unbridled power tucked within...that is the mark of a very special kind of warrior indeed."

As the room's energy seemed to reset, the grizzled teacher rolled her shoulders with a fierce grin.

"So then, Miss Elkins - what other surprises do you have in store for an old woman like me?"

"An old woman?" Casey couldn't help but retort with a grin, still coming down from the adrenaline rush of unleashing her volatile rei abilities. "Jeet, you can't be more than 10 years older than me at most!"

The master raised an eyebrow, seemingly amused by the playful jab. The others looked on with bated breath, wondering if Casey was about to find herself on the receiving end of another humbling lesson.

"Oh? And just how old do you think this 'old woman' is then?" Jeet asked, hands resting lightly on her hips.

Casey sized up her teacher's petite yet tone physique, trying her best to gauge Jeet's age through the haze of sweat and lingering rei distortions.

"I'd hazard a guess you're no more than 40 years young," the young fighter declared with a confident nod. "Which makes you barely a decade my senior at best!"

The assembled students watched Jeet carefully for her reaction. The diminutive martial arts expert regarded Casey stoically for a moment before throwing her head back with a hearty laugh that seemed to fill the training room.

"You cheeky thing!" Jeet grinned once her mirth subsided. "I'm afraid your rei senses need a bit more fine tuning. This 'old woman' has seen over 60 revolutions around the sun!"

Gasps of surprise and disbelief echoed from the peanut gallery. Even Aidan looked up from his computer screen, jaw dropping slightly at the revelation of Jeet's true age. For her part, Casey could only gape wordlessly, reassessing everything she thought she knew.

"What...? But how...you don't look a day over -"

Jeet waved her sputtering protest away breezily. "The mastery of one's inner energy is the fountain of youth, my dear. Now that you've glimpsed the vast potential simmering within you, perhaps you can start to fathom just how deep the well of rei power truly goes."

Resetting into a combat stance, Jeet's eyes danced with Challenge.

"So...shall we continue exploring those untapped depths of yours? I may be over the hill by your metric, but

I've still got a few more eye-opening tricks to show you!"

Jeet eyed Casey with a slightly bemused look as the younger woman processed the truth about her age.

"What, did you think these finely sculpted muscles and cat-like reflexes were some sorta parlor trick?" she scoffed, giving her bicep an exaggerated flex. "I've forgotten more about rei disciplines than you babies have even glimpsed!"

Before Casey could formulate a retort, Jeet burst into motion - her strikes a buzzsaw flurry targeting the young fighter's vitals. Each blow pinged harmlessly away at the last moment, but the palpable force behind them was undeniable.

"Getting...a little...carried away...with the...old lady...routine?" Casey managed to quip between desperately parrying and dodging Jeet's systematic deconstruction of her defenses.

In response, the elder master pivoted into a blindingly fast kata - her very arms and legs blurring into refractive shields of channeled spirit force.

"Let's go, runt! This old lady's Hailstorm Armor ought to show you what a true master can summon!"

With a bark of exertion, Jeet's ki erupted into a tempest maelstrom of hyper-compressed air pressure around her slight frame. The localized tornado howled with the ethereal fury of focused life energies taken to their zenith.

Casey could only gape at the unstoppable elemental

forces swirling around her mentor. Jeet allowed herself a thin smile amid the whipping vortex.

"What's the matter? Didn't you want to glimpse the 'untapped depths' an old relic like me can still plumb? Class is always in session, baby girl!"

A bead of sweat rolled down Casey's brow as she regained her breath from Jeet's explosive display of the Hailstorm Armor technique. Even after that awe-inspiring show of the master's power, the young fighter couldn't stop the defiant grin from spreading across her face.

"Hah! Is that the best an 'old relic' like you can muster?" she shot back, deliberately using Jeet's own mocking words. "With all due respect, Master, I think your age must finally be clouding your senses."

The other students tensed, expecting swift reprisal for Casey's brazen retort. But Jeet merely arched an eyebrow in silent challenge, daring her to continue.

Nodding with satisfaction, Casey fell into a combat stance, essence flaring around her fists already.

"You said it yourself - I'm just starting to tap into the raw, unbridled power inside me. So why don't you put away those fancy kata for a bit?" Her expression softened briefly with genuine fondness. "Let this 'baby girl' show you what she's got when she really cuts loose."

For a moment, Casey's eyes flicked to where her friends stood watching raptly. Aidan, Ken, and the others who had been her family for so many years. Her promise to them was clear.

"I'm done holding back anymore. Time to embrace the full force of my rei...and shatter through any limits you think you've got on me!"

With that declaration, Casey's spirit aura detonated in a blazing torrent around her slight frame. The sheer, searing intensity of her energy caused the air to warp and undulate like a mirage of primal energies suddenly given form.

If Jeet was surprised by the ferocious build-up, she showed no sign - simply shifting into a ready stance as her own focused essence sparked to life in response. Master and student regarded one another through the haze of catalyzing forces about to collide.

A heartbeat of silence fell...then with twin cries, they launched themselves into a clashing, brilliant eruption of unchained martial fury!

The air seemed to distort with the raw forces catalyzing between student and master. In the blink of an eye, Casey and Jeet had crossed the space separating them - trading rapid-fire blows that shattered the air with percussive detonations of rei power.

Even as the dojo's walls shook from the impacted exchanges, nobody present could peel their eyes away from the maelstrom of fists and elemental fury. Jeet's form was a blur, effortlessly weaving around the torrent of Casey's assaults while landing pinpoint strikes that crackled against her rei aura.

Just when it seemed the master was about to inevitably overwhelm her pupil, Casey's expression set into a rictus of pure concentration. Drawing from wells of potential she scarcely understood, ethereal flames erupted along her forearms in tandem with each blocked blow.

Crying out with exhilaration, the torrential barrage redoubled - forcing even the venerable Jeet to give ground under the relentless deluge of empowered strikes. For a moment, student had surpassed master as Casey's unbridled essence detonated around them in earthshaking percussive waves of pure...

...Halfway across Polkville, Tommy's hidden training facility shuddered as if from distant explosive detonations. Several of the gathered fighters actually stumbled, instinctively raising defensive guards before realizing the disturbance was external.

"What in the hell was that?" Chris demanded, shooting a look towards their impassive leader.

Tommy's jaw tightened imperceptibly as whispers of familiar power washed over his senses. Beside him, Joseph too felt the resonating forces and went still.

"It seems our old friends have been stoking the fires of their power as well," the grandmaster murmured, betraying little emotion.

Surveying his assembled trainees with cool calculation, Tommy allowed a cruel smile to spread across his face.

"Then it's a good thing we won't be holding anything back in our preparations either. Not if we want a shot at extinguishing those flames for good..."

With a subtle hand gesture, the Relic System around his wrist pulsed with blinding energies - banishing lingering doubts as its archaic mechanisms hummed fully online once more.

"Listen up!" Tommy barked, beckoning his pupils forward with palpable menace. "I don't care what sort of rei parlor tricks Kwondo thinks she's teaching those rejects. You're about to make a leap into mastering forces far beyond their quaint philosophies..."

As if in answer, the Relic System's aura engulfed the room in blinding crimson light, causing even Joseph to shield his eyes momentarily. When it passed, Tommy's wicked grin made the reason for his zealotry clear.

"Obey without question, and I'll show you all just how much REAL power I've claimed as my birthright!"

The path had been laid. Two opposing sides, equally determined to achieve transcendent martial mastery through willpower and rei manipulation alone...or by plundering the forbidden might of archaic forces man was never meant to wield.

Only one path could prove victorious when their inevitable clash finally arrived. On the streets of Polkville, the stage for that fateful conflict was rapidly taking shape.

CHAPTER ELEVEN

T wo weeks had passed in a whirlwind of fervent preparation. But as the crowds began flowing into the Polkville Grand Arena, the air seemed to thicken with palpable tension. This was the moment reality would finally intrude on the dueling visions being forged behind closed doors.

From the lavishly appointed locker rooms, Alex Ruler could feel the growing electricity resonating through the very walls. Settling into a meditative stance, he visualized the path of tranquil focus that had led him to this crossroads. Every sacrifice, every ounce of his being poured into embodying the Tiger Style's essence - it all culminated here.

"You ready for this, bro?"

Tai's voice cut through the silence, his presence radiating a contrasting aura of coiled intensity. Like the Dragon style he embodied, Tai was poised on the knife's edge between serene control and unleashed fury.

Alex opened his eyes, allowing his focus to expand

and attune to the seven other signatures accompanying them in the preparation area - Ken, Casey, Larry and the rest of Jeet's personally trained elite pupils.

"We were born ready," the Tiger stylist stated with iron conviction. "Tommy's deluded if he thinks he can just plunder his way to the power we've cultivated."

A loud roar from beyond the walls made the entire structure shudder - a harbinger of the maelstrom to come. Sharing resolute nods, Alex led his teammates towards the arched egress and into the blinding stadium lights.

Across the immaculately laid fighting ring, another faction was making their own entrance from the shadows. Tommy Leons swept his chilling gaze across the capacity crowd, allowing a heartbeat of silence before raising his arms in a grandiose gesture of absolute certainty.

"People of Polkville!" he boomed into the hushing din. "Witness and despair, for you are about to bear witness to a higher echelon of martial truth!"

With a subtle flick of his wrist, the Relic System's bloody aura flared with blinding menace - causing bewildered gasps and cries of alarm to ripple through the masses. Even Alex's group reflexively dropped into defensive postures as the archaic tech's dissonant harmonics washed over them.

"No more childish indulgences of mystical mumbo-jumbo," Tommy declared, his own pupils - Joseph, Chris, Vince and the others - flanking him with cold purpose.

"Starting today, we'll show you TRUE masters of the relics and how far determination BACKED by POWER can elevate the human condition!"

As a hush fell over the arena, the two distinctly aligned factions faced off from opposite sides of reality itself. Disciples of traditional martial arts mastery through mind, body and spirit, against a ruthless vanguard claiming to have uncovered the forbidden ways of transcending such limitations altogether.

The grand tournament to decide Polkville's future had officially begun. But the scope of this opening confrontation hinted at stakes far exceeding that of a simple civic clash of cultures. When the final blows were struck, nothing less than the dominance of polar philosophies would be decided.

****

The sounds of the roaring crowd faded as Alex squeezed his eyes shut, steadying his breathing. This was it - the moment he'd prepared for. He could envision Chris Dean's brutish form stalking out.

"There you are."

Casey's voice made his eyes open. She was standing beside a achingly familiar figure - Alyson, Alex's ex-girlfriend and former high school sweetheart, looking frailer but resolute on her feet.

"Aly!" Alex breathed, his heart clenching at seeing her out in public, recovering from the attack that nearly stole her from this world.

In two strides he pulled Alyson into a fierce embrace as Casey looked on with shining warmth and understanding. Alyson had not only given her blessing for Alex to pursue new romance - she considered Casey a dear friend herself now.

"You never could stay away from trouble, could you?" Alyson murmured at last, managing a tremulous smile as she released Alex.

He fought his own tears, struck by her resilience and strength. "Wouldn't be me if I didn't have a few guardian angels watching my back."

Casey stepped forward, taking Alex's hand firmly as she met Alyson's gaze. The three friends, bound by history, love and resolute purpose, savored a beat of calm beforeThe oncoming tempest.

"We're with you to the last, Alex," Casey stated, representing their unified ferocity. "No one gets to threaten our home, not while we're still standing."

Alyson nodded, placing her hand over their joined ones in a symbolic pact. "You two take care of each other out there...and pour every ounce of your fighting spirits into protecting what matters most."

As the opening bell clanged like fate's gong, Alex pulled them both close in a final embrace. Alyson's warm certainty...Casey's glorious fire...it would all fuel his azure blaze when he stepped into the maelstrom.

"Thank you...both of you. Wish me luck?"

"You won't need it, Rebel," Casey grinned, pressing her brow to his as Alyson watched with brilliant tender affection. "You've got something way better - us."

Squaring his shoulders, Alex raised his rei and strode out to meet Chris Dean's towering frame

****

The second Alex's feet hit the hallowed ground of the tournament ring, his senses achieved a preternatural sharpness. Breathe in, breathe out - his surroundings seemed to bleed into focus with each measured inhalation.

Across the expanse of finely raked sand, Chris Dean stood hunched and sneering - all brutish muscle and scar tissue. But Alex's heightened perception revealed the subtle inconsistencies. The fine tremors along Dean's knuckle lines. The fractional weight shifts concealing anxiety.

Good. Let the meathead relic-worshipper feel intimidated. Alex thinks to himself.

With a subtle flourish, Alex sank into a perfectly centered stance, his right hand trailing in a loose fist as ethereal coils of azure rei swirled around his forearm, taking the indistinct shape of claws.

Elongated, spectral facsimiles of a tiger's rending talons now sheathed his fingers and wrist. Even from his position, Dean's eye twitched as he registered the ethereal manifestation.

A hush fell over the capacity crowd as the combatants measured each other through the distortion of colliding martial auras. Alex knew he couldn't let this become a slugging match. His rei reserves, while vastly amplified through years of cultivation, still paled compared to the endless wellspring Tommy's flunkies could tap with their tainted Relic power.

No, this had to end swiftly and decisively. The key would be applying the Tiger Style's flowing forms to dismantle Dean's formidable defenses, channeling his rei strikes through those ghost-like claws to amplify their potency.

A strand of muscle along Dean's shoulder twitched - the slightest precursor betraying when he'd lunge. Alex tensed, coiled like a spring as his opponent's aura finally snapped into an explosive charge, only to have the larger fighter's silhouette warp and distort, as if passing behind a cosmic funhouse lens! Dean seemed to bifurcate, divide and splinter simultaneously in different potential trajectories and-

Alex's Eye of the Tiger ability blazed into brilliant focus. Cutting through the illusory fog, he instantly diagnosed the true path of assault and adjusted his counter.

Dean's relic-augmented speed only carried him partway through his cross-body bull rush before he found himself stopped dead - Alex's clawed fist impacting his sternum with the percussive force of a meteorite strike! Ethereal energy shocked outwards in refractive waves as the decisive blow found its marking.

The relic-empowered combatant's charge transformed into an inelegant pinwheeling stagger. But Alex had already flowed around his passing guard. Three measured inhales triggered three more lacerating claw arcs that detonated against Dean's plated shoulders and lower back like bomb bursts.

Wild, bestial aggression met with uncanny control and precision. There was no room for ego or showmanship, only pure submission to the Tiger's flowing forms.

And like a panther bringing down a raging bull, Alex Ruler kept pouring unhittable strikes through the path of least resistance until, with a final crest of energy...Chris Dean crashed face-first onto the sands, rei-shredded and insensate.

For a long beat, the only sound was Alex's controlled exhalation as he banished his talons and stepped back into a neutral stance. The larger man's aura frittered away like so much wasted potential.

And just like that, the opening salvo had been fired - the Tiger had bared its fangs, and the husk left behind now bore their lacerations!

****

Tai's breath came in controlled inhales and exhales as he visualized the imminent clash. Across the arena floor, Vince Raymon's lumbering frame already waited - eyes glinting with bestial hunger behind Tommy's tainted influence.

A soft rap against the locker room door shattered Tai's trance. His head whipped around as the portal cracked open, revealing an achingly familiar silhouette framed by a halo of fiery scarlet tresses.

"Kylie..." he murmured, drinking in the sight of the willowy young woman.

Kylie Grimes stepped fully inside, her warm green eyes shining with the same brilliant inner radiance Tai had first fallen for in high school. Poised and confident yet empathetic to her core, she was every inch the remarkable woman-to-be the teenage genius had promised.

"Hey there, kung fu fighter," she replied with a small smirk, crossing to take his hands. "Thought I'd wish you luck before you went out to, y'know...save the city and all."

Tai felt his chest constrict at her gentle teasing, an ember of youthful longing flaring after so many years of favoring the path of the warrior's discipline over all else. Here was the dream he'd forsaken to don the dragon's mantle - the pair's fractured high school romance abruptly cut short by destiny's inexorable call.

"Kylie...I don't even know where to begin-"

She stopped his words by boldly pressing two fingers over his lips, eyes now shining with unshed emotion.

"You don't have to say anything, Tai. I was there, remember? I watched you make the noble choice to follow your family's legacy into the mystic arts." Ducking her head, Kylie exhaled a tremulous breath. "Even if it took you away from me."

Something in Tai's chest unlocked at her plaintive honesty. Moving on pure instinct, he closed the distance to cradle her beautiful face in his calloused palms. Kylie met his intense gaze readily.

"This is about more than just upholding my ancestors' code now," Tai stated, pure conviction thrumming in every syllable. "Tommy's path is a perversion - a shortcut to power that spits in the eye of everything the Dragon Discipline embodies."

Kylie nodded, seeming to draw strength from his oath. "Which means today, tomorrow...however long this fight takes...you have to pour every ounce of your spirit's fire into driving that creep into the ground. No holding back, no hesitation."

"I know," he murmured thickly. "Which means I have to be willing to sacrifice...everything."

Despite herself, Kylie's eyes welled over at the magnitude of all he was resolving to potentially give up for this greater purpose. Gripping his wrist tightly, she shook her head fiercely.

"Not everything. You hear me, Tai Kwondo? There are some things worth clinging to no matter what inner inferno you're about to brave!"

And with that, she surged up on her tiptoes to crash her lips against his in a soul-searing, desperately overdue kiss! For an eternal heartbeat, the world fell away as warrior and dreamer became entangled - expressing every unspoken longing, hope, and unshakable promise in that ferocious bond.

When at last they broke apart, Tai's chest was heaving and his entire being felt somehow...lighter. More focused and centered than he'd been in a lifetime of inner exploration. Kylie held his gaze, her own radiant despite the glistening tears now escaping.

"That's your tether, Tai," she murmured, the conviction in her voice strong enough to anchor tsunamis. "When everything else goes to ash in the fires ahead...that's what you come back to. What you protect, no matter how insane the costs."

Tai could only nod, struck mute yet utterly resolute. As the opening bell's thunderous clang resounded, he turned and strode out to meet his opponent - and whatever brutal gauntlet lay beyond.

But now, Tai carried Kylie's talisman deep in his soul's core. An inextinguishable spark to cut through any darkness the road ahead dared put in their path!

Tai watched Kylie's retreating form disappear through the locker room door, her brilliant spirit seeming to cast a warm glow even in her wake. He lifted two fingers to his still-tingling lips, scarcely able to believe the soul-searing revelation that had just transpired.

The harsh sound of a throat ostentatiously clearing snapped him from his reverie. Whirling, Tai found Alex leaning against the doorway, an all-too-familiar Cheshire grin playing across the younger man's features.

"Well, well...if it isn't the Zen Master of the Drunken Lip-Lock style," the Tiger Stylist quipped, blue eyes dancing with undisguised mirth. "I was wondering when you two crazy kids would finally stop dancing around the obvious."

Despite himself, Tai felt his cheeks flush slightly as he attempted to regain some semblance of composure. "I don't know what you're talking about, Ruler. A warrior must stay focused and-"

"Oh can it, Kwondo!" Alex laughed, striding forward to deliver a playful shove against Tai's shoulder. "You've been tangled up in knots over Kylie since we were kids. About damn time you manned up and reminded her how us martial artists do it!"

The two friends regarded each other for a moment, chuckles subsiding into shared acknowledgment of their bond. Then Alex's expression softened as he reached out to grasp Tai's forearm firmly.

"I'm serious though, brother...I'm happy for you both. If anyone deserves to find some light amidst all this darkness, it's you and Kylie."

Tai nodded mutely, fresh determination filling his chest alongside Kylie's lingering warmth. "Thanks, Alex. And just so you know..." He flashed a wry grin of his own. "I plan on doing a lot more than just kissing the next relic-toting meathead that comes my way!"

Alex barked out a laugh, clapping Tai's shoulder

as he started to turn back towards the arena's entrance tunnel. The two martial artists moved in tandem, each feeding off the other's conviction.

"That's what I like to hear! Let's go show Tommy and his freaks how you discipline a dragon, brother. No more holding ba-"

The words died in Alex's throat as a slight figure stepped across the threshold into their path. Kylie blinked owlishly between the two men, seemingly unsure how to react to the intensity crackling between them.

"Uh...am I interrupting something here, guys?"

Alex shot his oldest friend a warm, if slightly sheepish grin as Tai looked on in wry amusement.

"Not at all, Ky. Just discussing the finer points of pugilism with my esteemed colleague here." He aimed a playful wink at Tai before turning to fully embrace Kylie. "You better have the ice packs ready, though. We're about to go scorched-earth on Tommy's whole operation..."

Chuckling, Kylie returned the hug with ginger care - a reminder of her own recent brush with violence. As she released Alex, Tai swept in to press a chaste kiss against the crown of her head, savoring her radiant warmth.

"Both of you just watch yourselves out there, okay?" she murmured, switching her gaze between the two martial artists turned guardians. "Keep each other safe and end this insanity."

"You know we will," Tai replied resolutely. With a

final nod towards his brother-in-arms, he turned to stalk out onto the arena floor - Kylie and Alex watching his departure with shining belief.

As the crowd's roar swelled once more around the imminent clash of skill and ideologies, one thing had become clear amidst the chaos:

No matter how apocalyptic the battles looming ahead would become, Tai Kwondo - and all his allies - now had a brilliant light to fight their way back towards when the smoke cleared. And that beacon would blaze brighter than any corrupted relics Tommy could ever hope to wield!

****

The roar of the crowd seemed to distort into a dull roar as Tai centered himself, eyes locked on the hulking figure already awaiting him across the ring. Vince Raymon cut an imposing silhouette, raw brutish power given form in knotted muscle and cold calculation.

But Tai knew all too well that the man facing him now was little more than an avatar - a puppet dangling from the strings of Tommy's corrupted influence. The Vince he'd once called friend had been systematically broken down, reforged into a vicious weapon yoked to serve a singular driving ambition.

No more. Today marked the line where that dark kingdom's reach was finally halted.

With an exhale, Tai swept his feet into the opening Dragon stance, chi already pulsing in cadence with his meditations. Reality seemed to bleed and distort ever so slightly around the focused fighter as his internal energies thrummed into harmonic onset.

Raymon's brow furrowed, lips peeling back from gritted teeth as he no doubt registered the first ethereal tendril of Tai's nascent draconic aura coiling around his frame. Good - let the brute feel the stirrings of powers he could scarcely begin to comprehend.

Another centering breath triggered the full release of Tai's fury. Twin pillars of scintillating emerald essence erupted around his fists with the thunderous concussive force of a starship's thrusters engaging! The arena's ground cracked and buckled underneath the gravitonic riptides of Tai's unleashed chi as he seamlessly transitioned into his most aggressive form - The Raging Typhoon Dragon!

Raymon barely had a chance to react before his opponent's form seemingly... fragmented into uncounted afterimage shards. Tai had already opted to open the dance by shattering the bonds of linear motion!

A staggered triple-blink of the former pit fighter's eyes failed to track his opponent's location. Then, with a noise like thunderclap, Tai rematerialized directly above and behind him - twin emerald-blazed meteors dropping in a high cross facsimile of the dreaded Dragon Ascendant!

Other masters might have aimed those empowered cestus-strikes at the obvious targets - kidneys, spine, the base of Raymon's skull. But Tai had never been one to lean on crude bludgeoning. No, his opening gambit carried far more insidious weight.

The first meteor-fist detonated against Raymon's right axillary bundle with bone-buchingForce - crude relic enhancements be damned! Even as shocked agony lanced across the larger man's face, Tai's second scintillating comet drove into the opposite deltopectoral grove with anatomy-shredding precision.

For a frozen moment, the only movement came from vapor tendrils leaking from Raymon's paling lips. Then his entire upper body seized and seemed to TWIST from the amplified whiplash of Tai's localized strikes against the nerve clusters!

"Arggghhh!" The agonized bellow tore from the former pit fighter's chest as his limbs began to take on decidedly...unnatural angles and trajectories. Nausea and dizziness slammed into his mind like a cargo freighter hitting a rogue wavecrest.

Perversions of space and proprioception conspired to rob Raymon of his most primal senses. Gravity itself seemed to warp and dilate at uneven vectors, causing him to buck and lurch in desperation for any stable frame of reference. His frantic limbs flailed as tsunami waves of spatial sickness rolled through his cerebellum unchallenged.

Tai, of course, remained a deific oasis of serenity amidst the chaos he'd unleashed - watching impassively as debilitating nausea and vertigo rendered his foe blind, disoriented and utterly defenseless. One final emerald ghostfire wreathed fist impacted like a judge's condemning gavel before he dismissed the technique fully.

"Know your path ended the moment you surrendered your soul to those tainted relics," he intoned, already turning away as Raymon crashed into eternal darkness behind him.

"Mine is the way of harmony with all forces - savage and serene. Yours was always doomed to the howling oblivion."

As the referee's hand fell to signal his victory, Tai turned his focused gaze up towards where Kylie and the others watched with shining pride. There were darker challenges lying in wait, deadlier foes still to be reckoned with before this fateful day's chaos reached its crescendo, but for now, the Dragon's spirit remained centered and resolute as ever. The first ferocious licks of flame had ignited around Tommy's corrupted regime. And the Inferno would only continue to swell from here!

****

Ken Manson's chest heaved with exertion as he completed the final kata, sweat beading across his brow. Sinking into a centered horse stance, he allowed his turbulent ape-style aura to settle like a storm system finding eerie calm.

The familiar chirp of his phone sliced through the locker room's sounds of exertion and focused breathing. Frowning, Ken snatched up the device and felt his heart skip a beat at the caller ID.

"Paris? You watching from the diner's TV?"

The warm laughter filtering through the earpiece made his chest tighten despite himself. "Where else would I be when my favorite customer is about to take center stage, Ken-Ken?"

He could perfectly picture the radiant smile gracing her features - the same dazzling light that had first caught his impetuous teenage gaze across the diner's bustling dining room years ago. Paris Colmorgen, the grounded angel who'd stitched his heart more thoroughly than she'd ever know.

"Listen, I, uh...I don't have long before they call me up for my match," Ken forced out, tamping down the swell of emotion. "But I'm glad you're there. Holding the fort down."

"That's my job, isn't it?" Paris replied, the bemused affection in her tone visceral enough to penetrate dimensions. "Speaking of which, do you have any...special orders lined up for your triumphant return feast later?"

Ken blinked, a slow grin tugging at the corner of his mouth despite the rising stakes weighing on his shoulders. "You mean aside from the usual double order of sriracha-garlic wings to celebrate kicking some relic-tainted ass?"

"Ohh, ambitious! But I do so love indulging my most successful customers."

He could hear the approving smile as Paris's voice took on a more earnest timbre.

"Just...come home to me safely, alright monkey-boy? No matter what sort of whacked-out chi-fury gets thrown your way out there today, I need you back at the diner counter so I can shower you with affection afterward."

Ken swallowed hard against the lump forming in his throat. He'd known Paris nearly his entire life, but their bond had been slowly transcending the platonic since his return from overseas training. The words they'd both been shying from took shape on his tongue before he could rein them back.

"You know...after all this gets settled? After Tommy's forces are dismantled and Polkville is out from under that looming shadow?" He paused, steadying his voice with effort. "I was thinking you and I could grab that bottle of thirty-year Nikka from behind the bar and...y'know, figure out our next adventure together over a glass or two."

The pause this time stretched into a small eternity before Paris's richly amused tone sounded again, softer now.

"Ken Manson...are you finally working up the courage to ask me on a proper date? With romantic intentions and everything?"

His heart thrummed triple-time in his chest, the tournament's entire weight receding into sudden insignificance beside that simple, loaded question.

"Well...I mean, if that's something you might also be-"

"Just win this crazy thing today," Paris interrupted firmly, though he could hear the smile returning to soak her words in warmth and promise. "Then you can ask me about that bottle of Nikka yourself when you make it back to my diner in one piece, tough guy."

A thunderous roar from the nearby tunnel entrance signaled his imminent summons to the arena floor. Ken squeezed his eyes shut, drinking in the comfort and purpose of Paris's voice one final time before squaring his shoulders.

"You know me, babe - I'm nothing if not victorious."

As the call slipped away, Ken Manson exhaled a sidious breath and moved to collect his signature staff. No matter what sort of foundational techniques the legendary Joseph Bailey unleashed, no force would prevent the Ape-Style master's furious homecoming!

After all, he had a very special dinner companion waiting with the perfect victory toast on the other side!

****

The opening bell's thunderous clang still seemed to reverberate through Ken's very bones as he prowled into the arena, staff whirling in controlled arcs. Opposite him, the towering figure of Joseph Bailey stood in an unremarkable ready stance - living history tailored into human form.

"You face the cusp of the infinite path this day," Joseph intoned, basalt eyes glittering with implacable focus. "Victory...or the yawning oblivion that awaits all who reject enlightenment's inner radiance."

Ken couldn't resist a wolfish grin as his ape-style aura crackled to pulsing life around his woven frame. "Yeah? Well this 'infinite path' you're hawking better be a damn smooth ride, oldtimer!"

With that, he exploded into a blinding combination of whiplash staff-strikes and bestial claw-hand counters. An elaborate rending overhand tree-truck sequence hammered in from alternating anglesOnly to disperseagainst Joseph's flickering afterimage as if it had never existed!

"Wha-?!"

"You fight with primal fury - admirable in its way," the wizened master's voice seemed to echo from every direction at once. "But untethered from insight and higher harmony, such brute force merely scatters futilely."

Ken's eyes widened as he registered Joseph phasing back into this dimension behind him, arms whipping out in a devastatingly precise volley. The first trio of impacts detonated across his exposed flanks like grenades, their shockwaves reverberating along every meridian pathway.

"But true mastery lies in guiding any force, no matter how primal or refined, through perfect union of mind and spirit!"

Responding on pure instinct, Ken funneled his ape-style intensity into a spinning tornado sequence - his staff and limbs blurring together into an impenetrable weaving helical spiral. For a beat, Joseph's metaphysical barrage ricocheted away from the maelstrom of Ken's unbreakable guard.

Until, with a subtle pivot, the legendary fighter seamlessly redirected his symphony of fists and footstrikeschannelingalongthe spiraling axis itself! His arms seemed to elongate, striking peripherally through seams of negative space never meant to exist!

First one unguarded meridian, then another withered under the inexorable pressures being threaded through Ken's ultimate defensive vortex. The young ape-style fighter's energies sputtered and distorted underneath Joseph's methodical dismantling - his entire life's studies undone by the application of a higher understanding.

Soon, the ancient's meditative cadence reached its inevitable crescendo - a picturesque rising double palm strike lancing out to crash against Ken's very center like the wrecking ball force of the cosmos itself!

All at once, his inertia screeched to a halt. Ken felt his control over every finely honed principle that had elevated him among Polkville's elite go shuddering away into oblivion. A strangled gasp escaped his lips even as the mighty staff clattered from his lax grip, followed by a ghastly crimson bloom spraying out across the arena's sands as internal ruptures catalyzed.

Through a creeping gray haze, Ken registered the sound of a baying roar - no, make that two - in the instant before his consciousness winked out entirely. But then only blessed darkness remained.

In the eye of that shadowed chaos, Joseph calmly rested back into neutrality, his expression betraying no hint of satisfaction or judgment. Merely serene contemplation as medical staff rushed to stabilize the trauma he'd inflicted upon the younger combatant.

"There are still two more stages on the arduous journey back to perfect harmony for all," he murmured, turning away as Tai and Alex exploded into the arena, the latter practically melting ground beneath his incandescent aura.

"Tiger and Dragon, your path grows ever more treacherous from here..."

Ignoring the frantic efforts to resuscitate Ken, Alex speared Joseph with the molten force of his baleful glare. His right hand clenched until knuckles paled, ghostly azure rei crackling up from clawed fingertips.

"Don't worry, you colossal son of a bitch," the Tiger Stylist snarled through gritted teeth, each word brimming with conviction. "Kwondo and I have blazed a trail of our own crafting on the way to granting your 'perfect harmony!'"

Joseph held his gaze steadily, unblinking in the eyewall of Alex's wrath. "Then after today, boy...only ash and echoes will remain."

The gauntlet thrown, the lines forever etched. For behind those clashing titans swirled elemental forces now rising towards an extinction-level escalation!

****

The acrid tang of cauterized blood hung thick in the air as Tai and Alex half-carried, half-dragged Ken's dead weight from the arena floor. The young ape style fighter's face was a rictus of shock and agony, shallow breaths wheezing from his ruined ribcage.

"Easy, easy!" Alex hissed through gritted teeth as Ken's battered frame jostled with each lurching step. "We've got you, brother. Just keep breathing..."

Medics rushed to meet them halfway, extending a levitating gurney to stabilize their fallen comrade for transit. Despite Joseph's clear control, the grievous internal traumas he'd inflicted were extensive and traumatic.

Ignoring the frantic personnel clustering around the emergent situation, Tai found himself locking eyes with Alyson where she stood pale and shaken in the locker room's entrance. A single glance conveyed the terrible gravity - Ken was in crisis, and there was nothing to do but wait for the healing team to work their craft.

As the medics whisked their patient away, a hush fell over the cramped space. Alyson sagged against Casey's shoulder, biting her lip hard enough to draw blood. Larry, Aidan and Keith all watched on in taut silence, the taste of ashes lingering bitterly.

Then, Ken's eyelids fluttered with monumental effort, anguished gaze locking onto where Alyson remained propped against Casey.

"P...Paris..." he managed to croak out around the

coppery mixture flooding his esophagus. "Need to...call her..."

Alyson   blinked, a sob catching in her throat as she pushed off from Casey to lurch forward towards the gurney.

"Ken! Ken, stay with us now, you hear me?" She gripped his trembling hand with desperation. "Don't you dare check out before you get to have that victory dinner! Paris is gonna be so pissed if she has to eat those stupid wings alone."

Despite everything, the ghost of a smile tugged at Ken's bloodied lips. "Not...letting that...hot bread down," he murmured with infinite gentleness before the medics sealed the gurney and whisked him towards the waiting medevac transports.

Tai had unconsciously migrated to Alex's side during the chaos, falling into their old training stances out of sheer muscle memory. Scarcely daring to breathe, he felt the Tiger Stylist's shoulders rise and fall in a shuddery cadence before speaking.

"Tommy and Joseph...they want to meet the Tiger"s Fury?" Alex's voice dripped with menace potent enough to sublimate diamonds under tons of pressure. "Well buckle up, because they're about to catch these thundering TALONS full in their smug faces! Nobody puts my family down like that!"

On cue, ghostly azure chi contours erupted around the young fighter's clenched fists - intricate carvings forming cruel hooks and vicious serrations along the knuckle ridges. His entire frame blurred and elongated, taking on a distinctly predatory cast as primal energies harmonized into unified accord.

Tai knew the signs all too well - those were the opening resonance signatures of his brother's ultimate Tiger Style Form.

He met Alex's molten glare steadily, emerald dragon fire already corona-blazing around his own aura in readiness. There would be more bloodshed before this tournament's conclusion, more escalations threatening to breach the barriers maintaining order...

But Tai and Alex's path would also burn brighter than ever before. No matter what profane echoes Joseph and Tommy unleashed, nothing could divert the two martial artists from achieving transcendence through focused totality of their art!

No more restraint. No more holding back their full warrior's essences from manifesting before this corrupted world!

As the medivac's engine roar faded into the distance, the locker room seemed to inhale a collective breath. Whatever frayed threads of stillness remained were about to detonate into all-consuming conflagration!

On the ash-strewn field ahead, the Tiger and the Dragon were about to awaken in all their terrible, unshackled glory...and the cosmic scales themselves would tremble against their earthshaking footfalls!

The medevac's engine drone finally shrank into

the distance, taking Ken to receive emergency care after Joseph's brutal onslaught. An uneasy silence hung over the locker room as the gravity of their fallen comrade's condition settled in.

Alyson was the first to shake off the stunned pall, lifting her red-rimmed gaze to meet Alex and Tai's steadily. Despite her pallor and lingering tremors, her voice rang out clearly.

"You two heard Ken - Paris needs to be with him when he wakes up. And after everything that's happened..." She swallowed hard, squeezing her eyes shut briefly before reopening them with new resolve burning in their depths. "After everything, he shouldn't have to be alone right now either."

Casey stepped up beside her, draping a supportive arm around Alyson's shoulders as she nodded in solemn agreement. "We'll go on ahead and meet the medevac at the hospital. Keep constant vigils with that hard headed warrior until he's back on his feet."

The two young women shared a look laden with unspoken history and unbreakable sisterhood. Then as one, they turned to Alex and Tai, everything premised in that shared gaze.

"You guys just take care of the ugly business still waiting out there," Casey stated, her fingers tightening almost imperceptibly around Alyson's shoulder. "Put that monster Tommy down once and for all, no matter what depravities he tries flinging your way."

"We're leaving Ken's legacy in your hands now,"

Alyson supplied, managing a wan smile that somehow still radiated endless caring warmth. "And we have complete faith you'll make his sacrifice a distant echo on the road to victory."

For a suspended moment, the two pairs studied one another through the hanging tension and unspoken galvanization. Larry, Aidan, and Keith watched on in respectful silence as ancient spiritual accords reverberated between them all.

Then with shuddering exhales of pure conviction, Alex and Tai replied with simple nods of unwavering oath - to Ken, to their loved ones, and to facing whatever savage nobilities still awaited with the boundless ferocity of their disciplines!

As Alyson and Casey turned to gather their things, the two martial artists beckoned their remaining teammates closer with an unspoken summons. No more words were required between the bonded family of warriors.

The gauntlet was quite literally cast now, with stakes elevated far beyond the petty conflicts that birthed this tournament's opening salvos! Joseph's sadistic display had ripped down the last veils of decorum shielding them all.

A line had been crossed in indelible streaks of viscera that could NEVER be undone or walked back.

Only one path remained now - to rain untold devastation upon the smug soul who'd shattered their fellowship so callously! No code would be respected, no restraints observed when the final reckoning at last erupted!

Alex Ruler and Tai Kwondo would become the unapologetic engines of a vengeance transcending mortal scales. Their respective Inner Beasts were all but loose, thirsting for catharsis against the Relic System's profane horrors!

And as their most treasured loved ones strode off to bear vigil over their fallen brother...the two Avatars turned to face the arena's egress with quiet finality.

All that remained was to become the purifying storm that would scour Polkville's boundaries with the ultimate lancing strike!

Whatever Tommy or Joseph hoped to awaken through their relic-fueled transgressions...they were about to summon something far darker and more primeval than even their foulest nightmares could conceive!

CHAPTER TWELVE

The opening bell's clang seemed to reverberate through the fabric of reality itself as Tommy Leons prowled into the arena's edge. Barely a flicker of movement preceded the instantaneous collapse of distance - one second the pit fighter Eric Jenkins was settled into his corner...the next he found Tommy's vise-grip around his windpipe!

"Did you really think I'd waste even a sliver of the relic's true power on insignificant vermin like you?" Tommy's words dripped with palpable disdain as his fingers constricted viciously.

Jenkins's face turned a splotchy purple as howling for oxygen, his already limited skills and conditioning rendering him helpless against the inexorable boa constrictor squeeze. Every desperate buck and thrash accomplished nothing beyond fueling Tommy's sneer of contempt.

With a dismissive flex, the Relic System's crimson aura engulfed the chokehold - its ominous harmonics vibrating at a fraying, sub-basilar frequency that caused the surrounding sands to shiver and roil unnaturally. A hairline network of fractal lacerations spread across Jenkins's mottled features as the bangle's energies siphoned away his ebbing life force.

"You're just the meager opening salvo on my path towards true ascendance," Tommy stated flatly, ignoring the other man's gurgling whimpers as his grip became an annealing vice of transdimensional forces. "Nothing but the faintest whisper to announce the coming oblivion I'm unleashing!"

With a subtle twist of his wrist, the Relic's resonance spiked to a teeth-rattling crescendo. Its bloody incandescence washed over the combatants fully...

...revealing Eric Jenkins caught in a rictus of shock, his body rapidly desiccating like an insect trapped in searing amber! Bulging eyes withered into sunken husks, while flesh and musculature calcified into an organic rictus of eternal torment. Stark horrors materialized as death's final rattling gasps were plied away from the unfortunate soul.

Yet Tommy stared into that hellish petrification impassively. His expression remained rigidly neutral as he studied (and ultimately discarded) the results of the Relic System's localized Vangeria distortion with clear indifference.

"A pity you held back even as your tortures commenced," he stated flatly while pivoting on one heel to face the viewing stands. Raising his voice to a bellicose register that carried across Polkville's breathless spectators, Tommy's delivery took on a distinctly unsettling timbre.

"Let that be your first harbinger of what happens when relic-empowered TOTALITY is grasped without pathetic qualms or self-deceptions!" he boomed from the heart of the desiccated zone spreading like a blight across the arena floor.

"Joseph may indulge himself by toying with outmoded philosophies and fancies...but I have NO SUCH RESERVATIONS when it comes to extinguishing those who stand in my path!"

As if in answer, the Relic System flared once more, its bottomless hunger pulsating through the city's foundations in primal, seismic echoes of oblivion beckoned. The first faint cracks began spider webbing across nearby structures as Tommy's grandiose gesticulations ratcheted up his unrestrained power call.

"Face the truth, coddled masses!" he snarled with full malevolence directed towards the milling crowds. "Not just your petty martial traditions, oh no...but the fundamental coordinates of your quotidian existence itself are about to be...eclipsed!"

With a final flourish, Tommy's hand swept upward in a motion that seemed to tear open the sky itself. Immediately, a spiraling cosmic distortion vortex erupted outwards in a cascading shockwave - buffeting the stadium's transparent shield walls and beginning to draw in scattered debris and particulate matter!

All throughout the structure's ancillary sections and stands, spectators scattered in abject panic, terror overcoming their deeper reasoning as raw violence on a cosmological scale was so casually being invoked. Hysteria quickly followed as the mini-singularity expanded, becoming increasingly difficult to maintain containment around.

Yet through it all, Tommy Leons stood as still as a statue, his eyes burning with unslakable hunger while surveying the bedlam around him. His lips parted in a thin, satisfied smile moments before his chilling declaration pierced through the maelstrom:

"Watch well, cowering filth...for this is but a MOTE of the oblivion to come if I'm further denied what is mine!"

With that, he slashed his hand downward in an imperious cutting motion. At once, the spiraling singularity pinched into nothingness with a resonant CRACK that rattled the arena's foundations. All across the bowled crater rapidly expanding from its epicenter, wisps of exotic radiation and outlier trans-dimensional force continued eating away at the formerly immaculate terrain.

As the haze cleared, it revealed a singular figure standing within the event horizon's wake - utterly unmarked despite having unleashed something that reduced reinforced plastisteel transparent shields to so much irradiated slag. Tommy Leons' casual display had served its purpose...to allow Polkville's blind masses to GLIMPSE the true depths of his relic-augmented sovereignty!

Without a single further word, the master

transgressor turned and exited the arena floor, leaving horrified silence and unmistakable destruction in his wake. Only vile intimations remained about what unshackled measures might follow when he encountered genuine opposition ahead...

****

As the echoes of Tommy's wanton desecration still reverberated through Polkville's foundation, a hush gradually settled over the rattled spectators. From the ingress tunnel, two solitary figures emerged – Douglas Kincaid striding forth with measured paces while his opponent Franz trailed several steps behind apprehensively.

The disparity between the two combatants was pronounced from their opening stances alone. While Franz postured with the jerky over-corrections of a brawler more accustomed to improvised melees, Kincaid's form flowed like a relentless river current. Muscles tightened and shifted beneath his traditional gi with an economy of motion speaking to decades, if not lifetimes, of cultivated practice.

When at last the younger fighter dodged an opening probing jab, Kincaid's counter materialized with blurring swiftness. One second occupying the center of his centered horse stance...the next detonating that solitary extended fist back upon itself in an unstoppable vector!

The deflecting 'uchi-uchi' parry didn't simply divert or smother Franz's untrained blow. Instead, Kincaid's technique catalyzed the law of energic percolation with nigh-supernatural dexterity! Like a whisper reverberating into a thunderclap, the tremor focused through his opponent's punching limb flowered into full-blown structural imbalance in the space of two stuttering heartbeats!

Almost in slow-motion, Franz's entire frame convulsed with the violent release of kinetic stasis transmuted force. Bones slipped free of alignment with melon-deep thuds, while tendrils of carmine blossomed across straining musculature from compounded shearing trauma!

An agonized bellow escaped the younger man's pale lips...only to trail off in a wet gurgle as Kincaid flowed seamlessly into the next stage of his transcendental kata. His opposite arm blurred with intricate torque geometry before a simple, almost gentle, palm impacted Franz's compromised centerline with sledgehammer finality!

The resulting percussion detonated internally, catastrophically redirecting the compounded momentum Kincaid had systematically cultivated from the opening exchange. In the span of a mortal exhalation, Franz's frame jackknifed into a grotesque forced contortion as the full might of his OWN unrealized potential rebounded through his fragile vessel!

For a frozen moment, the only movement came from the bloom of visceral crimson misting around the vanquished combatant's form. Then like a cruel puppeteer severing strings, that unbreakable knotwork of control unwound to allow Franz's broken, evacuated husk to crumple into an untidy sprawl across the arena's sands.

Silence swallowed the stadium as Douglas Kincaid observed his handiwork dispassionately. No words were necessary to convey the consummate skill gap between them. No sermons or wisdom cloaked in pithy metaphysics - only the stark truth etched in blossoming agony and lost vitality laid bare.

His adversary defanged thusly, Kincaid raised one arm toward the viewing stands where Joseph and Tommy stood with respective contingents. Those seemingly innocuous movements flashed with subliminal chi permutations potently decrypted by sensitives...

'It begins here. The past masters' complacent reign over our Art's highest potentials is ended!'

As the referee signaled the brutal victor, Polkville had bore witness to but an aperture's edge of the cosmic apertures pried open by Kincaid's lineage. And once his own opening salvo stepped through that threshold, those dusty regimes Joseph and Tommy clung to would evaporate into historical irrelevance!

For nothing could gird their antiquated doctrines against the true praxis of focused cataclysm that was finally leaving its hermetic womb. The WAY OF THE FIST's highest and most transcendental summits were dawning anew...courtesy of Douglas Kincaid's bloody awakening!

****

The thunder of the crowd had barely subsided from

Douglas Kincaid's chilling display when the stadium's public address system crackled to life with a piercing tone. All eyes turned towards the central announcer's podium as the unmistakable figure of Steve Bertinelli, CEO of Bertinelli Industries, strode into the spotlight.

Instantly, a hush blanketed the arena as Polkville's most reclusive business magnate surveyed the masses through the lenses of his signature visor-shades. Though advancing in years, Steve carried himself with an almost rakish charisma and self-assuredness more befitting a paterfamilias of ancient Rome.

"People of Polkville," he began without preamble, his distinctive baritone carrying easily to every occupied section. "Events have clearly transcended the scope of mere civic squabbling over martial philosophies and disciplines..."

He paused, allowing his dire acknowledgment to resonate amidst the already charged atmosphere. When Steve continued, an edge had sharpened in his graveled tones.

"Which is why, as the primary corporate sponsor for this 'Strongest Under The Heavens' spectacle, I feel compelled to intervene with some...extenuating stipulations."

A susurrus of confused muttering rippled through the stands, though it quickly stilled as Bertinelli raised one hand imperiously.

"By my purview, two distinct contingents have emerged as paramount contenders for the tournament's definitive culmination." His hand swept out to indicate Jeet Kune Kwondo's assembled team arrayed to one side of the field. "On one front, we have the stalwarts clinging to outmoded paradigms and mystical pseudosciences in their pursuit of transcendent martial expression..."

Then his steely gaze shifted to Tommy Leons and the relic-augmented cohorts radiating menace from their opposing quadrant.

"And holding the philosophically antithetical position - the vanguard who have quite literally rent apart the shackles of such human limitations through their reembraced mastery of powers our crippled era had foolishly abandoned as profane!"

Another pause lingered as Steve seemed to privately consider those polarized extremes for a beat. When he proceeded, his words carried the weight of an Emperor's declared fiat.

"Therefore, I am amending the rules and match progressions as follows: In recognition of their established peerless talents and accomplishments, Alex Ruler is hereby seeded directly into the tournament's semifinal berth!"

A stunned silence momentarily swallowed the arena as those words' implications sank in. Steve allowed it to linger for only a moment before charging on.

"Which leaves two remaining quarter-final matchups to determine who shall join Ruler in that decisional tier:

The first - Tai Kwondo versus the grandmaster Joseph Bailey! Let their long-awaited crossing of paths determine which of the old and new disciplines shall endure meaningfully!"

Hidden micro-drones dispersed throughout the stands zoomed in on the intensely focused yet opaque expressions decorating those two warriors' features. Neither registered any discernible reaction beyond deep, centering breaths.

"And for the second quarter-final..." Bertinelli's voice took on a subtly darker timbre. "We have Douglas Kincaid - this tournament's first harbinger that our species' shackles are finally slipping free! He shall face none other than Tommy Leons himself, the embodiment of how far we have rent the fabric of our perceived cosmic limitations!"

A visible tremor rippled through the audience this time at the implications of that penultimate confrontation's stakes. Steve allowed it to swell and crest for maximum impact before bringing his declaration home firmly.

"Let this ultimate reckoning unfold without any remaining constraints or delusional half-measures, warriors! No more charades or feinted gambits cloaked in false piety - only an unflinching demonstration of how far your respective paths can transcend before one is rendered...EXTINCT!"

With a final theatrical flourish, Bertinelli spread his arms in a gesture of encompassing benediction.

Almost immediately, the giant hololith screens mounted around the stadium's peripheries shimmered into active uplink - each displaying an imposing graphic render of the freshly decreed quarter-final matchups!

As roars and howls of either cheering zealotry or horrified dismay reverberated through Polkville's shell-shocked populace, Steve fixed his steely gaze solely upon the two remaining titans at the epicenter of this cosmic paradigm shift.

For while the masses could only perceive black and white polarities - an either/or proposition about which path would persevere over the other - Bertinelli had already glimpsed the fractal truth shimmering just beneath reality's veil.

This was never about contrasting absolutist ideologies extinguishing one another in zero-sum victory. No, the entirety of this escalating anarchy merely heralded the opening thunderclaps...of a singular, churning oblivion about to swallow them all whole!

And with grim satisfaction, Steve Bertinelli realized he and his mysterious patrons had secured themselves a front-row witness to that ineffable cosmic finality at long last!

****

The opening bell's clang had scarcely faded before Tai launched himself across the arena like a human meteorite, emerald chi scorching along his wake as the Dragon's raging spirit combusted to life! Joseph met the furious charge with a solitary upraised palm - ancient eyes glinting with implacable focus.

Their collision detonated shockwaves rattling every tooth in every spectator's skull for miles around! From the hyper-compressed nadir of impact, kaleidoscopic nebulae of unrealized force bloomed outwards in fractal plumes dripping with half-formed infinities. For a crystalline eternity, the two eternal warriors remained frozen amid those churning elemental eruptions...

...only for the singularity to abruptly collapse inwards upon itself! One fraying moment later, Tai found himself crunched against the transparent shield perimeter with bone-shuddering force - splintering fractal auras still simmering in his wake. But even as the Dragon Style's rib-cracking agonies lanced through him, the young master remained upright through sheerest force of will.

"Now THAT'S commitment, kid!" Joseph's graveled tones rang with grudging approval as he reappeared to resume prowling his side of the arena. "Shame the old ways are shackling your ascent. We could do such glories together unfettered."

Tai answered with a defiant flicker of jade firelancing forth from his fists. "Funny, I was about to say the same about your hollow dogmas, old man!"

Like a thunderbolt, he flushed twin billows of force blazing forth to engulf Joseph's form completely. Yet by the time those meteoric detonations cleared, his opponent's figure had disappeared entirely into an artful enmeshment of emerald torrents!

"To glimpse the infinite and refuse its mysteries...weakens us all."

Joseph's whisper seemed to issue from every iota of distorted space refracting around his vanished coordinates. Dragon energies bucked and thrashed in frustrated torrents seeking egress from their containment field!

Then transdimensional singularities erupted across Tai's back and chest as the wizened fighter's fists punched through from shunted spatial trajectories never meant to converge in this plane! Cascading shockwaves of displacement trauma battered away the surging chi torrent entirely, leaving Tai nude and exposed as crimson bloomed across his flesh in lurid whorls!

"That's the difference between us," Joseph continued in that same unbroken murmur even as he moved with blurring swiftness to Tai's exposed side. "Your tradition only glimpses its shadow - while I have Mastered the Way fully!"

Strands of energy crackled around his upraised palms even as Tai whirled to meet his relentless assault. Their frames flickered and coruscated as trans dimensional barriers tore and shredded around them in the instant before another geometric implosion of force detonated!

This time, the combatants ricocheted apart to opposite arena quadrants, cloven away from the singularity birth in pinwheeling aftermaths of shredded auras and distortion echoes. Spectator shields strained as stray spatial disruptions lashed them.

Yet Joseph instantly rematerialized in a centered stance even as Tai staggered upright, his breathing reduced to ragged sucking gasps as every exhalation misted crimson vapors. Defiant fury burned from his storm-tossed gaze.

"You...can't break me that easily..." he spat through a tooth-clogged gurgle. "The Dragon's spirit burns...too brightly...to be snuffed out!"

With a war cry, he charged once more - this time foregoing restraint entirely as his verdant chi blazed around him in a supernova aura of pure, untrammeled force! Joseph's eyes narrowed as the entire arena seemed to tremble under that cosmic swell growing exponentially.

An instant before colliding again, the two lined their forms as if engaged in a symbolic ceremonial exchange of essence. Then with a detonating pulse of energy, they unleashed their respective ultimate techniques simultaneously!

Tai's spirit burned with the raw plasma fire of a Dragon Ascending ascendant form - unstable stellar energies coalescing around his frame in thermonuclear radiance! At the same time, Joseph's entire being fragmented into a blur of dismantled spatial coordinates held in kaleidoscopic tension. Each of his afterimage-limbs bristled with the scintillating event horizons of a million realities poised to intrude!

As the two ultimate exchanges clashed head-on,

the resulting detonations rattled foundations city-wide! Waves of force rebounded off the arena's transparent shield housings to ignite chain reactions of violent distortions cascading back inwards. Spectators scattered in abject panic as the universe itself seemed to be shredding asunder around the transdimensional fury engulfing the combatants!

Then with a reality-shattering crescendo, the twin omega techniques cross-catalyzed into a spiraling singularity implosion unlike anything Polkville had ever witnessed! Spheres of cosmic fire and negative curvature space tore apart the arena's ground, funneling into a vortex rapidly swallowing the entire venue!

In the nadir of that terminal event, two silhouettes could briefly be glimpsed - Joseph and Tai rendered as dueling iconographs poised at the very brink of oblivion's consummation! Inches separated their upheld hands, forces held in ultimate stasis as the last ebbing ripples of distorted order tried to hold existence itself together...

...but even that fragile binding could not endure indefinitely. With a thunderous snap-hiss, the infinite singularity vortex collapsed, both eternal disciplines expelled outwards beyond the arena's furthest perimeters in an apocalyptic fireball of realized thermal potential!

As clouds of ionized particulate misted down in the wake of such primal release, the twin masters appeared locked in their climactic stances - hovering in the burned fusillade between the arena's extinguished boundaries. For long moments, the only movement came from the smoldering vapors rising off their ravaged forms.

Then simultaneously, Tai and Joseph listed into unconsciousness, ruin incarnadine sprawling from opposite horizons beyond the destroyed venue entirely. In the silence that reigned over Polkville afterwards, only the certainty of this ultimate path's future lay preserved:

While the Tiger and profane Relics remained paths yet untrodden...the Dragon and the Way's escalation towards total cosmic breakthrough had finally been unharnessed and aimed squarely upon their next obstacle. Neither would relent until the remaining restrictions were shattered and transcendence achieved through apocalyptic severance!

For Joseph and Tai had gazed across the face of true oblivion this day...and found accord in rushing to meet that annihilation's untold mysteries with ravenous spiritual fire burning yet brighter!

****

The locker room's metallic door clanged open, admitting a battered and scorched figure that could barely be recognized as Tai Kwondo. Ragged breaths rattled from his chest as the Dragon stylist practically fell through the entrance, legs threatening to give out completely.

"Easy, easy!" Alex was at his side in an instant, ducking under Tai's leaden arm to support his wavering frame. "I've got you, brother. Just stay with me now."

Somehow, despite his mangled state, Tai managed

a wry chuckle that quickly deteriorated into a wet coughing fit. Crimson speckled across the floor between them as he fought for air.

"Joseph...is a warm-up act...compared to the next...levels..."

"Don't talk, you crazy bastard," Alex shot back without rancor, guiding Tai over to one of the benches lining the chamber. "Just concentrate on healing up and resting that dragon spirit of yours."

Gingerly, he helped ease his friend into a seated position, taking stock of the rampant trauma with a critical eye. Third-degree plasma burns across most of Tai's musculature...compound fractures along his supporting limbs...and hovering at the periphery, suggesting exotic radiation poisoning. It was a miracle he'd even retained consciousness after whatever unholy forces he'd unleashed against Joseph.

"I'm sorry, Alex..." Tai rasped hoarsely, wavering focus struggling to meet his brother's concerned gaze. "Couldn't...finish the old relic off...for you and the others..."

Despite the solemnity gripping him, Alex felt a rough chuckle rumbling up from his core. With gentle insistence, he gripped the back of Tai's neck - pressing their sweat-beaded brows together in the ancient warriors' bonding.

"Are you kidding me, you melodramatic idiot?" he murmured with fierce affection. "You just survived going past the event horizon of the infinite abyss itself...and walked back out the other side still burning!"

Tai's eyes widened fractionally at the acknowledgment thrumming through that simple, sacred contact. But Alex wasn't quite done yet.

"So don't you dare say you failed the team or anyone else, TK. Because whether or not you took Joseph down permanently..." His free hand rose to hover over the azure rei radiance sheathing his own knuckles in sharpened talons. "You lit the path that's going to allow me to stomp all over whatever horror this so-called 'way forward' summons next!"

As a tremor of rejuvenated vigor seemed to ripple through Tai's battered frame, Alex pulled back with a fierce grin blazing across his own features.

"Rest up and recover, Kwondo. Because no matter which sadistic freak emerges from that next arena - Kincaid, Tommy, or something even uglier - you and me are taking them apart together!"

Settling back, he aimed one final penetrating look at his best friend as emerald motes of incandescence flared off Tai's subtle nod.

"Just like we always swore we would...until one of our inner beasts lets out its final, purifying roar!"

The weight of that vow resonated between them, binding spirit to spirit through ties transcending traditional disciplines. Overhead, the locker room seemed keen in anticipation and hunger for the coming storm.

After all, one of Polkville's cosmic hunger to awaken was now inevitable. And when that cataclysm detonated in earnest, Alex Ruler would be howling from the very epicenter - his tiger spirit's fury aimed squarely at whatever profane eldritch horrors dared cross its path this day!

****

The arena floor seemed to reverberate with baleful harmonics as the twin monoliths of violence prowled towards its center. Douglas Kincaid moved with the eternal poise of a sculptor about to undertake his masterwork chisel strokes. Every step, every micro-readjustment of his centered stance channeled the full breadth of his lineage.

Opposite him, Tommy Leons radiated a far more frenetic aura - the sense of a caged primordial force scarcely restraining itself. His eyes burned with soulless hunger as the Relic System around his wrist pulsed in a staccato cadence synced to ultraterrestrial rhythms.

Despite himself, Kincaid felt his focus narrow to study that profane anomaly. He could sense the bangle's energies manifesting as scalar distortions across the visible spectrum, almost as if it were a localized rift into some blasphemous dimension beyond.

"You can stop gawking anytime, fossil," Tommy sneered, causing Kincaid's gaze to snap back with laser focus. "I'd have thought even Neanderthal rejects like yourself could recognize the future's pangs when they start eating away at your outdated delusions."

Kincaid refused to rise to the younger man's taunts. He knew the path of transdimensional mastery far too intimately to fall prey to such primitive projections.

"Bold words for one who has yet to part the veils and confront the ISNESS underlying all transitory states," he finally replied, relishing the minute tightening around Tommy's eyes.

As if in answer, the Relic System flared with scintillating infrablack/ultraviolet signatures ripping open gaps in the visible spectrum. Unleashed and shapeless terror seemed to pour in through those spectral lacunas - draping shredded patches of unrealized geometries and echoing resonances in their wake.

"And is that vaunted 'ISNESS' of yours terrified enough yet by the mere whispers of my birthright's TRUE VOICE?!" Tommy bellowed as those accursed waveforms began shattering the air around them.

"Because I promise...once our dance has truly begun...even your primordial nightmares will prove inadequate to fathom what I'm prepared to unleash!"

Almost as punctuation, the distortion geometries slashed outwards in ominous arcs - filling the air with Stygian smoke as they swept across the arena. In their wake, sections of fortified flooring were simply...gone. Cut away into void without any sane transition or comprehensible mechanism!

Yet Douglas Kincaid remained implacable, his piercing gaze never wavering from Tommy's blistering aura as even more reality breaches cascaded around them. Finally, he replied with a tone carved from transdimensional harmonics older than the Earth's core.

"Awaken the abominations of your ancestors all you wish, wretched scion. Some blessings simply cannot be derailed by chaos' last, fading tantrums before the silence rebirths itself anew!"

At that, Tommy's temper rabidly combusted with a detonation of pure hate! His immediate aura spiked with distortions far more virulent than anything the Relic's preliminary warmup had teased.

"In that case, I'll just have tear the sickly vestiges of your 'silence' down to its primordial molecules so it can't delude itself about rebirthing EVER AGAIN!"

His final syllables erupted as a gravid roar even as the Relic System pulsed out an aberrant slipstream of recursive superscission tendrils! They whipped outwards in harrowing lashes of annihilation entropy hell-bent on atomizing everything in their path.

Rather than attempt to evade, Kincaid sank deeper into his stance - feeling his chi meridians unlock with symphonic accord as the Way of the Fist's innermost sanctums welcomed the assault wholeheartedly. Hands whipped out to engage those ultraomnicidal filaments mid-termination...only to initiate a geometric choreography of precision sublimation!

Where Tommy's lashings sought the profane termination of all patterns through chaotic superimmersions, Kincaid's inverse articulations coaxed their virulence into cohering back towards simplexes, dividing and recomposing the raging nullities into holistic primes!

Soon, their diametric exchanges reached a screaming fever pitch - slipstream infinities smashing against counter-manifold inceptions with percussive impacts birthing entirely new standing wavefronts spanning multiple dimensional strata! Neither side could gain dominance over the other as the arena birthed itself into an obscene cyclone of energized realities and searing transcendental geometries churning ever inward!

Yet still the dervish escalated further and further, with both Kincaid and Tommy achieving quantum-fired states of omnicausal hypercertainty! Each microsecond saw their chi manifesting into hyperspheres with impermissible boundary conditions...only to have them recursively collapsed and reconstituted into spawning new cosmic substructures!

From the stadium's outer sections, only Bertinelli's rune-forged occult projectors allowed limited glimpses of the infinite Golgothar playing out on elysian grids strung across all celestial axis permutations. The endless, hellish genesis-rebirth-extinguishing cycles birthing whole realities and antiverses with every reciprocal exchange!

What felt like both a fractional nanoinstance and hyper-eternity of eternities battered away, only terminating as the impossible nexus of churning geometries reached a catastrophic crescendo of Planck frequency transgressions!

Slingshotting through these infinitesimal singularities, Tommy's final virulent entropy slipstream lanced forth from a subatomic defect with ludicrous overbaking!

Only to find Douglas Kincaid's masterfully cohered manifold geometry awaiting as its transcendent solution and final resonant counterpoint across eternity itself!

For less than an ephemeral instant, a fleeting new boundary condition was imposed - one where all possible causal structures twinned along a singularly mirrored trajectory spanning ALL holistic states!

Reality itself paused seemingly unable to decide which transfinity to birth into next...

...until the entire infinitely reducible emanation reached its final simplest harmonic divisor and unified closure in the shape of a singular well-worn fist!

Under exionically folded metrics, that final kinetic singularity terminator slammed forth with synchronized percussive impact surpassing any cosmological cataclysm or big crunch/bang! Fractal harmonics arranged their devastating termination payload through Tommy's vaunted Relic disruption shells.

They crashed home with fate-shattering force, detonating one final transcendent finality as the last echoforms of every unrealized dominion collapsed into itself...

...ERASING Tommy's consciousness outright from existence itself!

For a few eternal seconds thereafter, the arena remained scorched and frozen in undisturbable stillness.

Then with an earth-shattering crash, Tommy's vacant biomass cratered down into a smoking heap of ash and cooling slag.

As if emerging from a deep fugue, Douglas Kincaid inhaled sharply and turned to face the crowd with an expression of deep, cleansing satisfaction.

"Thus will all those who foolishly court ruin's scream find only entropy's last whispered surrender before the Way's eternal truth!"

The words rang out with finality borrowed from stars shredding from their own quantum death rattles. And as they did, Bertinelli stepped forth once more into the arena's halo spotlight beams with a look of clear admiration.

"Ladies and gentleman, it seems we have witnessed the first definitive crossing of uncharted thresholds in preparation for this tournament's grand unravelings!"

Raising his arms to encompass the still-faintly crackling arena surface, Steve's next pronouncement carried the weight of biblical benediction.

"For on the morrow's eve, we shall bear witness to the final escalation, the ultimate collision course, when Ruler's inner savagery joins Kincaid's abyssal mastery in the last cataclysm before our world faces...Rebirth across new horizons!"

A single hand dropped to flick open a repeater control, immediately summoning med-evac units already prepping for what cataclysms lay in wait beyond that threshold.

"For tomorrow's exhibition promises to leave NOTHING holding itself back any longer!"

As the crowd's roars and screams reached new fever pitches, Steve allowed a small, grim smile to tug at his lips.

"And while the players strut and posture on borrowed stages...the universes they will all soon serve await with utmost indifference after all!"

With that, he strode off to see his masterwork realized at long last.

****

The air was thick with anticipation as Alex Ruler and Tommy Leons finally strode out to meet in the center of the battered arena floor. This was the crossroads all of Polkville's escalating chaos had inexorably led towards - the ultimate ideological collision between tradition's disciplined ferocity and the profane terrors of the reawakened Relic System.

As the two combatants assumed their opening stances, their auras blazed in diametric opposition - Alex's azure rei flaring in spectral contours around his clenched fists, while Tommy's crimson relic-fire seethed in eldritch, trans-dimensional eddies. It was clear from the outset that no quarter would be given, no boundaries left uncrossed.

The opening exchange set the tone for totality as the two forces collided with the explosive fury of a celestial Event. Shockwaves of unrealized potential detonated outwards in fractal geometry, shattering the very continuum around that apocalyptic nadir! Spectators scattered in terror as the arena itself began to warp and distort under the cascading resonance.

The tension was thick enough to choke on as Alex Ruler and Tommy Leons finally met in the center of the arena. The two warriors locked eyes, the timeless clash between Order and Chaos given living embodiment.

"Well if it isn't the great Alexander Ruler himself," Tommy sneered, breaking the silence as he began circling like a serpent. "You fancy yourself a paragon of truth and honor. But let's put those vaunted principles to the ultimate test!"

With a signal from his hand, Tommy's henchmen shoved Alyson and Casey forward at knifepoint. Both women were battered but defiant, their fierce gazes burning into Alex.

"Alex! Don't listen to his lies!" Alyson cried out in warning as she was forced to her knees.

Casey matched her step for step, refusing to break eye contact with the man she'd grown to love so deeply. Despite the punishing blows she'd endured, her spirit blazed brilliant and unbowed.

"You see, for all your noble posturing about sacred traditions and disciplines, you've got some attachments that are decidedly...unholy," Tommy goaded, drinking in Alex's anguished expression with sadistic relish.

"So let's exercise those lofty principles of yours in deed rather than just empty words! You can only save one of these women, Ruler. The woman who was your youthful dream? Or the new passion firing your bloodshed here today?"

Gesturing again, his men placed Alyson and Casey back-to-back - blades hovering inches from their throats in preparation for the cruel choice.

"Who will you renounce to keep walking your path, mighty warrior?" Tommy's tone dripped with poisonous mockery. "The virginal first love who grounded you? Or this fiery new spirit challenging you towards greater becom-"

"ENOUGH!" Alex's roar detonated like a thunderclap, stilling the arena into echoing stillness.

When he spoke again, his words carried a weight and conviction that seemed to bend reality itself around their fervent gravity.

"You can threaten whatever profane rituals or demonic pacts you wish, Tommy. But the path I walk transcends such puerile conceits of attachment or possession!"

Inhaling deeply, Alex swept his gaze between the two women with a look of blazing intensity. When he continued, it was with ceremonial solemnity utterly devoid of ego or agenda.

"Alyson was the spark that first allowed me to glimpse my inner fire's truth. The dream of an undying summer that fueled my passion's genesis."

Turning his full focus onto Casey, Alex's next words came edged with a revered tenderness usually reserved for sacred rites.

"While you, my fierce phoenix, became the forge tempering that youthful idealism into the purifying furnace it was always destined to become. Your spirit's gift opened my eyes to the eternal cycle burning away all illusions of limitation!"

Refocusing on Tommy's sneering disdain, Alex's entire frame seemed to resonate with cosmic power as his rei aura exploded into brilliance around him. When he bellowed his declaration, the very arena trembled before its finality!

"But any path claiming authority over what possible becomings the universe will allow is itself the lie! There are NO choices to be made where loves' ultimate potential is concerned...only the all-consuming conflagration that existence ITSELF was breathed into being to facilitate!"

With that, Alex's corporeal form appeared to dissolve into a towering spectral ziggurat of scintillating azure energies - the primordial Tiger Spirit's anthropo bionic aspect manifesting in all its terrible, cataclysmic glory!

Twin plasma contrails of unrealized thermal force slashed from the colossus' eyes to leaving the arena and cascading towards the bodies of Taison Kwondo and Kenneth Manson, pulling their spirits into Alex.

"Tigapagon Style! Tiger Transformation!" Alex roars.

Alex could feel the primordial essence burning within him, the Tiger Spirit raging to be unleashed in its full, terrible glory. He lifted his head, allowing the incandescent azure energies to blaze throughout every fiber of his being.

Strands of crimson light began weaving through his aura, streaking across his musculature like branching lightning. His body pulsed, shadows cast in strobic undulations as ancient metamorphic triggers embedded in his core activated in a chain reaction.

Throwing his head back, Alex bellowed in profound agony and rapture! The sound seemed to reverberate across dimensions - a call to issuance so primal it transcended mere vocalizations. Veins of fire burned beneath his skin as his mass rapidly densified, musculature expanding explosively.

Fell, bestial contours erupted across his frame as the Tiger made its presence known through his transfiguring vessel. Alex's hands clenched into cramped talons, nails elongating into glossy black serrations. A corona of smoldering emerald energies ignited around his forearms, refracting into phantasmal claws wreathing those re-forged extremities.

His shoulders mounted relentlessly as new biomass accrued in geometric expansions. Trapezius and deltoid gorges deepened into troughs of knotted, predatory sinew pulsing with unholy vigor. Even Alex's cranium seemed to elongate subtly in accompaniment with the jawline's restructuring - fangs protruding through his snarling rictus as facial features took on a distinctly feline cast.

Layer after layer of augmentation cascaded along his bodily nexus, remaking the very molecular structure into a seamless instrument of preternatural might and savagery. Scorching rushes of rei chi radiated from every pore, searing prismatic contrails in the confining air around the morphing colossus.

At last, growth parameters reached their apogee as the metamorphosis climaxed in a final thunderous detonation - explosive force rupturing outwards to scalp every surface in a ten-meter radius! As the shockwave's distortions settled, a fearsome new entity stood poised on the former arena floor's scorched crater.

Easily nine feet of densely-muscled mass draped in smoldering cerulean pelt, it cut an imposing aspect befitting the Tiger's most rarefied battle-trance. The towering apparition's smoldering emerald aura contours sheathed its entire frame in pseudo-elemental interference patterns, as if the very air struggled to interface with its refactored density matrices.

Upswept feral ridges framed its blazing cthonic aspects, while the lower torso's contours jutted into bestial extremities more befitting a crouched biomorphic siege engine than any remotely anthropoid anatomy. Even the distended cranial vault enforcing that rictus snarl betrayed anatomical restructurings warping beyond this reality's framing principles.

As it turned to face its adversaries, the ambient lighting of Polkville's arena itself seemed to warp and distort in discordant alignments. This was no mere trance-aspect or heightened combat phantasm - Alex Ruler's most primal essence had fully invested its eternal Tiger Spirit into redefining the limitations of a mortal corporeal instrument!

Existence itself had been restructured into a new ordering paradigm with that metamorphic detonation. And from the exultant, reverberating bellow echoing off every surrounding surface...this was only the primordial overture to whatever cataclysmic upheavals were inbound for any ill-fated enough to stand in its path!

The arena seemed to hold its collective breath as Alex Ruler towered over Tommy Leons' crumpled, scorched form. The transgressive archon who had unleashed such cosmic depravities lay frozen in a rictus of existential torment - his relic fires extinguished and charred husk drained of even the capacity for defiance.

Alex studied the broken shell of his former nemesis impassively for a long beat. Then, with ceremonial finality, he allowed the last vestiges of the Tigapagon aspect to blaze forth in one final obliterating technique.

Raising his right hand, ghostly azure energies coalesced around his fingertips - refracting into wicked, hooked talons of pure cataclysmic potential! Each flexing seemed to distort the surrounding continuum in sympathetic transductions, as if merely invoking this strike's cosmic lineage held notional reality itself in stasis.

When Alex finally shifted into the opening vector, his movements transcended the mortal context entirely. One heartbeat he stood aloft like an avenging deity...the next he was THROUGH that infinitesimal arc separating origin and eschaton entirely!

The Enigmatic Tiger Claw detonated against Tommy's ravaged form with the full, unshackled ferocity of primordial natural orders asserting their dominance! Gale-force contrails of thermal force bloomed in cataclysmic interference patterns, reducing the arena's air to turbulent eddies of ionized particulate!

With a thunderous concussive force, the omnidirectional shockwave expelled what remained of Tommy's vessel in a streak of indelible finality. His ruined husk sailed out towards the arena's boundaries to impact the shielded perimeter in a starburst of crumbled debris - broken and cauterized to immobility in equal measure.

For a frozen moment, Alex stood astride the cratered nadir left in his ultimate strike's wake. His chest heaved with exertion and metaphysical expenditure as the last thrumming distortion echoes finally settled. Finally, the young master allowed his corporeal form to revert back to its native aspect.

As ethereal energies shimmered away, Alex swayed on his feet - barely regaining his faculties before slumping into momentary unconsciousness. All around him, the devastation of the apocalyptic campaign stretched outward as far as the eye could perceive.

Yet in the spaces between that existential wake,

pinpricks of renewed truth glimmered with sacred promise.

"Alex!" Casey's voice cut through the silence as she sprinted into the arena, boots kicking up plumes of particulated ash. She slid to her knees at his stirring side, cradling the warrior's frame tenderly. "Alex, oh my god, you did it! You actually did it!"

"Of course he did," a second, quieter voice sounded from nearby. Alyson limped forward to crouch beside them both - reaching out to interlace her fingers through Alex's. "Did you ever doubt he would?"

Despite himself, a wan grin tugged at the corners of Alex's mouth as he drank in the sight of the two most important people in his entire universe silhouetted against the ruination and promise alike. It was the true sight he had fought to manifest all along.

"H-hey there, gorgeous ladies," he managed to rasp out through a grimace. "Sorry about the pyrotechnics show...girls dig tigers, right?"

Both women let out watery chuckles at his indomitable levity amidst the still-settling cataclysm, pressing their foreheads together atop his weary brow. For a heartbeat, the three radiated with simple, profound affirmation of their shared triumph over every ashen shadow and lingering oblivion.

Further back in the staging area, Keith and Larry stood watching in respectful silence - carefully binding the comatose Tommy in reinforced manacles. The criminal kingpin who had trafficked in cosmic nightmares was down for the final count.

As they moved to secure the prisoner for transport, Keith flashed Alex a grim salute of acknowledgment and pride. The indomitable Tiger Spirit had triumphed, safeguarding their world through the most apocalyptic trials. A new reality had been forged, shining with the luminous promise of higher becomings yet to unfurl.

In that eternal moment, their bond of fellowship seemed to transcend the dust and ashes of today's battles entirely. The road ahead shone bright with sacred truth and unshakable certainty - Polkville's protectors would walk those horizons with towering, undimmed conviction ever after.

No matter what profane echoes still stirred from the void's unsealed corners, nothing could stray the Tiger Spirit's ascendant path henceforth. Alex, Casey, and Alyson held that eternal flame's radiance deep within them all. Its luminous roar would resound across the stars themselves from this blazing overture of a new cosmic age!!

CHAPTER THIRTEEN

The morning sun peeked over Polkville's skyline, casting its brilliant rays across a cityscape forever altered. Though the physical rebuilding efforts were already underway, an ethereal pall still hung in the air - a lingering psychic reverberation from the cosmic cataclysms unleashed.

In the days since the Strongest Under the Heavens tournament's apocalyptic culmination, a hushed introspection had descended over the populace. It was as if the entire city were holding its collective breath, struggling to process the sheer scale of the existential upheavals they had borne witness to.

For Alex Ruler, the stakes felt even more visceral as he sat across from Alyson and Casey over coffee that morning. His ex-girlfriend turned closest confidant, and the brilliant new woman who had unexpectedly ignited his heartfire remained stubbornly by his side in the aftermath.

"You know, when you first started rambling about some underground tournament tearing the city apart, I figured it was just your overactive imagination running wild again," Casey remarked wryly.

Alyson chuckled, reaching to give Alex's hand a supportive squeeze. "I think we all massively underestimated the full scope of what you'd gotten yourself tangled up in this time, tiger."

Gazing into their caring eyes, Alex felt the weight of his exploits settling in with a renewed gravity. He had sacrificed so much - shattered so many inviolable premises - in his zealous pursuit to blaze the Tiger Spirit's path all the way to its blazing omega point. Could he truly say the incalculable losses and civilization-shattering upheavals were justified?

"I know the past few weeks have put you both through more chaos and terror than anyone should ever face," he began somberly. "Polkville isn't just another battleground to me - it's my home that I swore an oath to protect. And in my arrogance, my hunger to confront the abyss head-on...I led those profane forces straight into the heart of everything we hold dear."

The regret and self-recrimination welled up as Alex pressed on in a low murmur. "You two paid one of the heaviest prices through the collateral fallouts of my stubborn quest. Alyson, you nearly had your future snatched away just for the crime of loving me..."

He squeezed his eyes shut, forcing out the words. "While Casey, you were put through unimaginable torments, all because I couldn't resist the call to push my abilities to their limit, regardless of who got caught in the crossfire."

Alex's voice cracked with the weight of his burdens. What petty lies and delusions of destiny had he followed into depravity?

Then the softest touch grazed his cheek, sending shivers through him. Opening his eyes, he found Casey gazing with profound empathy and care.

"You can stop torturing yourself over the what-ifs anytime," she said, her voice solemn. "We're still here, aren't we? Front row witnesses to one of the most mind-blowing events this city has ever seen!"

"More importantly," Alyson chimed in with a wry grin, "we got to see the man we love most burn away every veil of illusion to reveal his truest essence. The part of you shining too bright for any shadow to diminish."

She rose to slide in beside him, wrapping her arms around his torso. "You became the eternal embodiment of the Tiger's promise, Alex. The part that could never be extinguished or turned aside, no matter what cosmic torments arose. That's what shields my soul."

On his other side, Casey mirrored the embrace, her affection radiant. "We're part of that primordial fire too. As long as we uphold that sacred light together, the darkness is powerless against our way forward."

At last, Alex's inner demons stilled. Gathering his loves close, he surrendered to their shared, unshakable affirmation.

He could finally glimpse past the cosmic battles towards the true prize - a world remade whole, blazing alongside the Tiger Spirit's ascendant path towards sacred reunion.

One way or another, Polkville's vigil over those luminous horizons had only just begun. And Alex vowed to walk that shining road with every fiber of his being, from here to eternity's end!

****

The private recovery room's ambient hush was broken only by the steady beeps and rhythmic whoosh of the medical monitors. Tai Kwondo lay unconscious, chest rising and falling in time with the respirator's cycling pulses. Jagged lacerations and mottled contusions adorned his face and torso - visceral testaments to the metaphysical cataclysms he had endured.

Slouched in the bedside chair, Kylie Grimes looked on with hollow-eyed vigil. Her hand remained entwined with Tai's, as if by sheer force of will she could transmit vitality into his battered vessel. Though streaked with tears, the young woman's expression remained stalwart as a matriarch shepherding her most precious charge through darkness.

"You've got to pull through this, Tai," she murmured, giving his limp fingers a reassuring squeeze. "The world still needs its Dragon Spirit blazing brilliantly to light the way forward."

Despite her own profound concerns, Kylie managed the ghost of a tremulous smile, thumb tracing the contours of Tai's clenched knuckles.

"And I still need you here with me so we can start exploring what destiny lies on the other side of those sacred fires you breathed to life."

A faint line furrowed Tai's brow at her tender tones, eyelids fluttering with subconscious effort towards consciousness. Kylie immediately leaned in closer, slender fingers combing the sweat-matted hair away from his noble features.

"That's it, Spyro...follow the sound of my voice," she crooned with a caregiver's soothing lilt. "Wherever the battles took you, you've got to find your way back to the truth awaiting us both right here..."

Nearby, a soft rapping on the chamber's door cut through the intimate moment. Kylie glanced up to find Paris entering, balancing a tray of fresh linens and packaged meal supplements.

The two young women shared a silent look of profound acknowledgment and care. Though things would never be as they once were, their respective beaus had bonded them through transcendent love's vigil over these cosmic days of reckoning.

"Hey there," Paris murmured, crossing into the room properly with a warm - if slightly strained - smile. "I brought some fresh supplies to help keep our boys on the mend."

Kylie returned the kindness with a gentle nod. "I won't be able to settle my soul until they're back on their feet, Paris. Not after everything they risked confronting those...dark tomorrows threatening to eclipse all we cherish."

Resting the tray on the bedside table, Paris reached over to grasp her friend's shoulder in a grounding squeeze. "Well it's a good thing us hometown girls have always been stubbornly rooted in the here and now, isn't it?"

The pair shared a commiserating chuckle at the wry observation. Turning her gaze back towards the heavily-sedated Tai, Kylie felt that steadfast inner conviction solidified anew.

"You're   right," she stated, voice thrumming with ceremonial promise. "We'll keep tending the sacred flames until every last lingering shadow has been banished from their souls. Then, when they finally awaken into the light..."

She trailed off, fingers trailing along the sharp line of Tai's jaw as she leaned in to brush her lips across his feverish brow - sealing the innermost wish blazing behind each loving caress.

"...we'll be there to show them the brilliant new horizons they've birthed into existence!"

Further down the recovery wing's corridor, much the same scene played out in Ken Manson's private room. The young ape style fighter's chest rose and fell in labored wheezes, his face a mask of enforced slumber shadowing against the pillows.

Unlike Tai, however, Ken's condition was far

more precarious. Joseph's metaphysical dismantling had rendered his internal systems perilously close to complete system failure. It was only through Paris' stalwart refusal to give up on him that he still clung to the mortal plane whatsoever.

Slumped in the bedside chair, the diner waitress looked every bit the exhausted all-night vigil-keeper. Dark circles hung beneath her eyes, the usual spark of effervescent personality muted amidst her all-consuming concern.

"You stubborn jackass," she muttered in a tone of profound affection, watching the steady rhythm of Ken's chest rising and falling. "Throwing yourself out there against monsters like that without a single care for your own safety."

Reaching out, Paris traced the ugly roadmap of contusions and plasma burns along Ken's jawline with a featherlight caress. Beneath her fingertips, she could feel the constant sub-harmonic thrumming of chi flows straining to stabilize his precarious condition.

"As usual, your spirit's fire burns too damn brightly for any limitations to contain it," she breathed in a lowing murmur, brow furrowing. "Just like when we were kids and your gung-ho attitude was always flaring up faster than I could douse the flames."

A tremulous chortle fought its way up from her tightening throat, Paris' free hand moving to pinch the bridge of her nose.

"You'd think after all these years, I'd know better

than to try and handle that inferno alone, huh Manson?"

As the tender confession hung in the still air, Ken's eyelids fluttered with visible effort - as if straining against the tonnage of his own depleted energies towards consciousness. Paris immediately leaned in closer, drinking in every labored inhalation and subtle microexpression rippling across his features like a shipwreck victim gasping for oxygen.

"That's it, tough guy," she encouraged, fingers brushing his matted hairline tenderly. "Follow the cadence of my voice and find your way back from that sanctum you waded so damn deep into this time."

Ken's nostrils flared, chest seizing with exaggerated effort as cognizance slowly crested behind the veil of sedation. Then, as if traveling lightyears through labyrinthine deeps of inner planes, his eyes abruptly shot open with startling lucidity!

"...P..Paris..." he rasped with a gurgling wheeze, instinctively seeking out her familiar grounding presence.

"I'm here, you big doofus," Paris assured, guiding his questing hand to cup her cheek. Though streaked with tears of relief, her own expression shone with profound solace and rekindled hope yet smoldering defiantly. "I'm not going anywhere until you return...ALL the way back from whatever sacred hells you waded into for me."

Despite the toll of his rei taxed across Ken's ravaged countenance, something flickered behind those iris pools

- a profound understanding catalyzed with the sublime epiphany:

While Tai and the other warriors may have blazed the Tiger Spirit's eternal promise across the cosmic battlefield...Ken himself had just glimpsed the primordial fires of devotion and reciprocity fueling those sacred quests from the other direction!

If anything could reforge him from the nihilistic ash of those tribulations, Paris' steadfast heart-flame would serve as the inextinguishable spark to light that arduous path onward!

****

The late afternoon sun cast stretching shadows across the park's grassy knolls as Alex, Casey and Alyson strolled along the winding footpath. Despite the peaceful setting, Alyson seemed to carry a solemn weight about her.

She drew in a steadying breath before finally breaking the silence. "There's something I need to share with you both."

Coming to a halt, she prompted Alex and Casey to turn and face her with inquisitive expressions. Alyson worriedly bit her lower lip momentarily before pressing on.

"I know the tournament's aftershocks are still settling...but I've realized I can't keep running from confronting my own inner tensions any longer."

Casey instinctively took Alex's hand, the two

sharing a concerned look as Alyson met their gazes.

"You both mean the world to me," she said, a tremulous smile tugging at her lips. "Alex, you've been my closest friend for so long. And Casey, seeing you embrace your own fierce spirit has been incredibly inspiring."

Alyson paused, visibly steeling her resolve before continuing. "But I can't keep denying the callings that have been stirring within me, pulling me toward growth I've deprived myself of for too long."

A crease furrowed Alex's brow as the implications dawned on him. "Aly...what are you saying?"

"During the tournament's escalation, when reality itself warped and fractured..." Alyson swallowed hard. "My sister Tiffani, who has been here in Polkville helping me recover from the attack, thinks I should travel with her a bit. You know get out of town for a while?"

"Just dont make it eleven years before you return," Alex blurts out, chuckling nervously.

Casey squeezed Alex's hand supportively as Alyson pressed on.

"Tiff didn't force me into anything. She simply...opened a path for me to finally confront the spiritual fires smoldering within that I can no longer deny after brushing so close to oblivion."

Unconsciously, Alyson took a step back - her energy field expanding with the gravity of her words.

"We all had our belief systems shaken and

reshaped, didn't we? You with your blazing Tiger Spirit path, Casey with her own rebirth..." Her gaze shone with bittersweet affection. "Well this is my wake-up call to immerse myself fully in walking the spiritual path."

The implication hung heavy before she laid it bare:

"I'm leaving Polkville for a while to travel and deepen my own spiritual journey. I don't know how long this will take..."

Her eyes pleaded for their understanding, even as her words carried finality.

"But I need you both to promise you'll look after each other - and this bond you're nurturing together - while I'm gone."

Casey immediately stepped forward, pulling Alyson into a fierce embrace as tears shone in her eyes. "We'll keep the lights on for you, Aly. I swear it."

As the two women held one another, Casey shot Alex a pointed look over Alyson's shoulder. After a long moment, the uncertainty melted from his features and he moved to join the embrace.

"Damn straight we will," he rumbled gruffly. "And you'd better leave one hell of a beacon to aim my Tiger Spirit towards whenever you're ready for me to come charging after you again."

Alyson let out a watery chuckle, holding them both tightly. "Don't worry, you two...I'll make sure there's always a path for us to converge again when the time is right."

As their shared laughter mingled in the dying rays of dusk, a sense of bittersweet tranquility settled over the trio. Changes loomed and separations awaited, but their connection would remain blazing brilliantly.

For Alyson, Alex and Casey already knew with unshakable certainty: No inner or outer odyssey could ever truly sever the eternal flames binding their kindred spirits across all planes and seasons yet to come.

As their shared laughter mingled in the dying rays of dusk, a sense of bittersweet tranquility settled over the trio. Changes loomed and separations awaited, but their connection would remain blazing brilliantly.

Polkville had been reborn into new cosmic destinies - and each of them would walk their respective paths faithfully until the cycle inevitably flowed them back into sacred reunion once more.

For Alyson, Alex and Casey already knew with unshakable certainty: No inner or outer odyssey could ever truly sever the eternal flames binding their kindred spirits across all planes and seasons yet to come.

Then, Alyson's expression wavered, the levity draining from her features as she stepped back, wringing her hands anxiously.

"There's...one more thing I need to come clean about," she said in a small voice.

Alex and Casey immediately sobered at her shift in demeanor. "What is it, Aly?" Alex asked, concern furrowing his brow.

Alyson worried biting her lower lip, struggling to meet their eyes as tremors started in her shoulders. "When...when you first came back to Polkville after being gone, I..."

She trailed off, visibly steeling herself before pushing on in a rush. "I got tangled up with Tommy and his relic-worshipping goons for a little while. They preyed on my fears after the attack and I...I betrayed your trust."

Fat tears rolled down Alyson's cheeks as the confession hung in the air. "I told them about your investigation, I gave them information that put you and everyone else in danger. I'm so sorry, Alex. I never wanted--"

She broke off in a choked sob, hunching in on herself. But Alex was already pulling her into his arms, cradling her shuddering frame against his chest.

"Shh, shh...it's alright, Aly," he murmured, rocking her gently. "We all got a little lost in the chaos for a while there."

Casey moved to wrap her arms around them both, lending her quiet strength. "What matters is that you found your way back to us in the end."

Alyson's fingers twisted in the fabric of Alex's shirt as she clung to him like a lifeline. "But I put you all at risk! I nearly ruined everything with my stupidity and fear..."

"No," Alex stated firmly, pulling back to cup her face in his calloused hands. His deep green eyes burned with conviction and caring as he held her gaze. "You listen to me, Alyson Jergens. Tommy Leons and his relic-cult were predators who exploited vulnerability with their mind-games and false promises."

He brushed the tears from her cheeks with tender sweeps of his thumbs. "What matters is that when it came down to the wire, when our family was on the line, you were right there standing alongside us against the darkness. That's what I'll never forget."

A fragile smile tugged at Alyson's lips as she reached up to cover his hands with her own, drawing strength from his words and Casey's steadfast presence.

"I don't know what I did to deserve you two idiots," she breathed with a watery chuckle. "But I'm grateful for it every single day."

Alex just grinned, pulling her back into a fierce embrace between himself and Casey. "That's the way it'll always be, Jergens. No matter what spiritual odyssey you've gotta undertake or inner fires you need to confront..."

He met Casey's shining gaze over the top of Alyson's head, feeling the words resonate outward in a vow older than the stars themselves.

"We'll be the ones burning brightest on the path to lead you home again when the time is right. You can take that sacred truth straight to the damned cosmos."

As the trio held each other under the twilit canopy, a sense of abiding peace settled over them. Their bond had been tested, stretched nearly to its breaking point...but the eternal fire that transcended all temporal concerns had seen them through to the other side, remade stronger than ever before.

No matter what wonders or terror awaited along the road ahead, Alyson, Alex and Casey would walk those luminous horizons with their spirits braided as one - an inextinguishable blaze to guide them inevitably home whenever existences' cycles split them apart for a breath.

The Tiger Spirit had forged them into sacred keepers of that primordial vigil...and no force in any cosmos could corrupt their luminous oath henceforth.

****

The penthouse office was cloaked in shadows, the floor-to-ceiling windows offering a panoramic view of Polkville's' glittering skyline. Only a faint glow emanated from the desktop monitor, casting stark chevrons of light across Antoine DeMarco's chiseled features.

The video call's connection light blinked a few times before resolving into the unmistakable visage of Steve Bertinelli, CEO of Bertinelli Industries. Despite the late hour, the corporate tycoon appeared impeccably composed.

"We need to accelerate our timetable," DeMarco stated without preamble, eerie shadows pooling in the hollows of his eyes. "With Leons' spectacular flameout at that farcical martial arts tournament, the market's ripe for realignment."

Steve arched an immaculate eyebrow but remained impassive. "You make a fair point. Tommy's apprehension has created...a temporary power vacuum in the region's street-level operations and distribution networks."

DeMarco's jaw tightened as he leaned forward, the dim backlighting throwing the hard planes of his face into stark relief.

"Temporary is right. Which is why I've already put contingencies in motion to solidify our position while that fool rots in lockup." A perfunctory hand gesture, and a video feed of Polkville's industrial district flickered onto the screen.

Steve's lip curled ever-so-slightly as the grainy footage resolved into the unmistakable sight of a heavily armed biker gang dismounting from their choppers. Their sleeveless leather cuts emblazoned "WENDIGOS" across the back in a sneering, jagged font.

"You can't honestly expect those mouth-breathing glorified squid to successfully leverage Leons' territories away from his establishment," Steve said with derision, lacing his cultured tones. "Especially against the coordinated opposition currently being rallied by Ruler and his rogue's gallery."

Rather than rising to the bait, DeMarco simply allowed a razor-thin smile to crease his features. "Let's just say I'm providing the Wendigos and their allies with some...elevated chemical incentives to maximize their efforts' success."

With a few taps, the footage transitioned to a new video - this one depicting an underground laboratory humming with illicit activity. Figures in hazmat suits moved among it's an elaborate array of chemistry equipment and manufacturing apparatus.

"I call it 'Thrush'," DeMarco purred with undisguised satisfaction. "A highly addictive and potent cutting-edge amphetamine analog to our legacy products. It also causes transmutations within its users. Which is why only my inner most circle of The Wendigos get to truly test it. "

Steve's eyes narrowed as he studied the operation with a practiced eye. "You've weaponized your formula, elevated its addictive potencies to untenable extremes..."

Another thin smile, this one radiating sinister promise.

"Exactly. The Wendigos' foot soldiers will essentially become neurally-bonded berserker agents - unstoppable fiends driven to exsanguinate any opposition by our salesforce's superior product."

Onscreen, a figure in the lab hunched over an open tray - carefully manipulating hypodermic instruments to administer concentrated doses to the thrashing forms of what looked like feral human test subjects!

Steve observed the scene with an inscrutable poker face. "And the human costs, colalteral damages?"

Now DeMarco allowed the full menace of his predatory gaze to bear down, teeth glinting like fangs as he bared them in a bestial leer.

"All necessary growing pains to solidify our expansion into Polkville's markets, Steve-O. Leons underestimated our product's potential to inspire blood-soaked synergy...but I can assure you, my Wendigo Shock Troops won't be so limited by archaic scruples or restraints."

The two arch-criminals sat regarding one another through the video uplink, unspoken acknowledgments of their respective ruthlessness and appetites passing between them like a crackling static charge. At last, Steve gave a single imperious nod of assent.

"See that they don't disappoint then, Mister DeMarco," he stated with all the finality of a judge's gavel strike. "We're committed to elevating our business to an entirely more...detached paradigm now."

As the call disconnected, DeMarco allowed himself a deep fortifying inhalation before pivoting in his chair. The panoramic windows offered a breathtaking vista of a Polkville modest skyline shimmering in the distance - a veritable Canaan of virgin markets and potential elevation into the big leagues.

All he needed were the right scourges to wrest that promised land's control from Ruler and his vigilante confederates. And once his Wendigos embedded their Thrush supply across every city block, no force would rival the delirious bloodletting they'd unleash to solidify their new dominion!

Antoine allowed a fresh predatory grin to crease

his aristocratic features as he raised his tumbler in a private toast.

"To new empires violently risen, and promising darkness reclaimed..."

CHAPTER FOURTEEN

The thrum of neon and the siren song of chiming slot machines filled the smoky air inside Tommy's Wild Cherry Casino. Laughter and raucous cheers echoed off the garish scarlet walls as patrons milled around the packed gaming floors.

All that cacophony died in an instant when the entrance doors exploded inward with a deafening concussive bang!

"This is the Polkville Police Department! Everyone stay calm and make your way to the exits in an orderly fashion!"

Alex Ruler's commanding bellow cut through the stunned silent as he stalked in flanked by Aidan, Keith, Larry and a squad of heavily armed officers. The Tiger stylist moved with purposeful strides, an azure aura already flickering to baleful life around his right fist.

"All casino employees and personnel are hereby

instructed to remain in place and surrender!" he continued, sweeping his fiery gaze across the sprawling establishment. "We have warrants to bring you in under charges of racketeering, extortion, and a massive list of other offenses carried out under Tommy Leons' leadership!"

The civilians scattered in full panic at Alex's bellowing announcement, surging towards the side exits as quickly as self-preservation allowed. Only a knot of familiar, hardened faces stood their ground - including one particularly repugnant character positioned behind a high roller's booth.

"Well, well...if it isn't the reigning king of street trash himself," Marcus Bagwell sneered from the confines of his wheelchair, pockmarked features twisting into a rictus of hatred. "I was wondering if we'd get to revisit just how far the so-called 'Tiger' is willing to go in the name of that law he loves polishing so vigorously!"

Casey, positioned just behind Alex, felt the warning tingle of his rei energy spiking dangerously. "Easy, Ruler. This skell ain't worth compromising your own code over."

"She's right," the former pit fighter rasped on, undeterred. "After what went down between us last time, you really think I wouldn't take a few precautions just for you?"

"You're right, Marcus - we do have some unfinished business remaining between us. More than enough for me to exercise appropriate force if needed."

The venom in Alex's words hung heavy, daring the wheelchair-bound criminal to make one wrong move. Marcus's pockmarked face twisted into an even deeper sneer.

"Hah! You think I don't know all about how you operate, Ruler? Using brutality and mind games to get what you want, no matter who gets crushed underfoot."

He leaned forward as far as his battered frame would allow, eyes burning with hatred.

"My brother Brutus was just your latest victim in that rampage, wasn't he? Lying in a hospital bed somewhere, another casualty of the so-called 'Tiger's Justice!'"

Casey tensed beside Alex, feeling his rei energy spike dangerously at the accusation. Before he could respond, she stepped forward - her own fiery aura flickering to life.

"That's enough out of you, dirtbag!" she snapped, emerald flames dancing along her fingertips. "You really think we don't know the kind of depraved freakshow Brutus was mixed up in with Tommy and his goons?"

Marcus recoiled slightly at her vehemence, but the sneer remained firmly in place.

"Oh I heard all about the big tournament showdown, little girl. Where this self-righteous thug wasn't a fighter enough, so he had to cheat by unleashing some kinda crazy alien power-up just to stand a chance!"

He jabbed a finger towards Alex, who had remained stock-still and impassive throughout the accusations.

"That's the kind of monster we're dealing with here, officers! One who will stop at nothing to impose his flawed idea of 'justice' on anyone who gets in his way. Even if it means warping himself into some kind of demonic freakshow like Tommy and the relics!"

For a long moment, Alex held Marcus's seething glare. Then finally, he let out a slow, measured breath - his aura settling back into a tranquil flow.

"You're right about one thing, Marcus," the Tiger Archon stated, words carrying an weight beyond the venom. "My path did require me to achieve a higher state during the tournament. One where I could finally shed every last constraint and delusion barring my spirit's truest intensity."

Raising his right hand, azure rei contours shimmered around his fingers as they elongated into wicked crimson talons. The officers instinctively tensed, rifles pivoting to track the display of metaphysical power.

"But you're dead wrong if you think that transcendent focus was anything like the depravities Tommy and his masters trafficked in," Alex continued, letting the ethereal energies play across his aura. "This is the gift...and burden...of the Tiger's most ferocious aspects finally unleashed upon a reality that's allowed corruption and malice to fester for far too long."

Taking a step forward, he stabbed his taloned hand

towards Marcus - stopping just short of the cowering criminal's face.

"So ask yourself this, 'friend' - are you truly deluded enough to believe your warped understanding of what I've become could ever withstand being on the receiving end of my path's ultimate dismissals?"

The threat hung heavy in the air, leaving Casey and the other officers to weigh the potential cost of pushing Alex too far towards that savage precipice. For his part, Marcus seemed to shrink back slightly - the fire dimming in his gaze as indecision warred with hatred.

The standoff stretched onward, both sides momentarily frozen...until finally Alex lowered his hand and the tension broke. Turning his back to Marcus, he addressed the assembled police unit.

"Get this trash processed and into holding. We'll deal with his delusional ramblings in a court of law, as is proper."

With that, he began to stride away - leaving a visibly shaken Marcus Bagwell to wrestle with the fact that, as always, the Tiger of Justice moved with principled conviction even when staring into the face of ultimate necessity...

****

The aroma of Eunice Ruler's famous pot roast wafted through the cozy kitchen as Alex stepped inside, instinctively inhaling the comforting scents of his childhood home. Rounding the corner, he found his mother fussing over the oven while Casey chopped vegetables at the counter.

"There's my heroic son!" Eunice looked up with a warm smile as she caught sight of Alex. "You're just in time to set the table for me."

"Yes, ma'am," he replied easily, crossing to gather the stacks of plates and utensils. As he worked, Alex couldn't help stealing glances at Casey - so at ease amidst his family's home. Her hair was pulled back and she moved with a practiced grace, occasionally singing along to the music playing from the living room.

From the hallway, the sounds of raucous roughhousing and laughter echoed as Alex's teenage nephew Chase barreled in. The lanky youth barely avoided colliding with his uncle before skidding to a halt.

"Oh man, I thought you'd never get here!" Chase grinned up at Alex with unabashed admiration.

Rolling his eyes good-naturedly, Alex ruffled the boy's hair. "Don't you mean you're just excited for one of my infamous strategy breakdowns over dinner?"

"Something like that," a new voice sounded as Alhan Ruler entered the kitchen, his eyes crinkling with mirth as he pulled Alex into a brief, fierce hug.

"It's good to have you back under this roof again, son," Alhan said gruffly, trying and failing to keep his voice from wavering with emotion.

A moment later, Amy Davis - Alex's older sister and Chase's mom - breezed in carrying a fruit salad, giving

Casey a playful nudge.

"Well aren't you two just the perfect little housewives today?" she teased. "Who knew the big tough Tiger Warrior and Firestarter had such domesticated sides?"

Casey laughed as Alex feigned indignation. "Hey, I worked up an appetite wrestling the entire criminal underworld into submission this week!"

The family's playful banter flowed easily as they all migrated to the dining room table, settling into their usual seats like patterns etched by time itself. Joining hands, Alhan cleared his throat and bowed his head reverently.

"For this meal, and for the countless other blessings surrounding us once more, we give thanks. May our bonds of love and honor only strengthen further with each new day's dawning..."

As his father's words washed over the gathering, Alex allowed his gaze to roam from face to face - taking in his incredible support system. He saw the woman he loved matched only by the miracle of having her by his side through every unrelenting trial. The rock-steady foundation of parents who'd shaped his moral bedrock without wavering.

His partner's steadfast presence, though physically absent, resonated powerfully. The nephew who looked at Alex with the same admiring eyes he'd once turned towards his own martial arts idols all those years ago. And his big sister, Amy, living embodiment of persevering through profound loss to still stand tall.

When Alex's eyes finally found Casey's across the table, he saw her returning his look of wonderment with a radiant smile and a subtle wink. A whispered promise that this - the quiet moments of peace, fellowship and unconditional acceptance - was the true reward awaiting at the end of their shared path.

As Alhan finished the benediction, Alex raised his glass towards the center of their gathering.

"To persevering through every crucible," he said simply. "And to never losing sight of what matters most along the way."

The family's answering echo of "Hear, hear!" resonated outward, carrying unshakable conviction into the warm spring evening.

For the Ruler legacy would endure long after the dust of any one battle had settled - an eternal wellspring of courage, honor, and the abiding belief that true justice came from fiercely protecting the essential humanity in us all.

No matter what malign forces dared rise against that truth in times ahead, the Tiger's roar would remain unified with his chosen family in their sacred vow to honor the deepest spiritual wellsprings.

Those eternal verities wouldn't simply withstand every attempted profanity and injustice inflicted upon the world...

...they would emerge burnished anew and more

brilliantly radiant than ever against the fading light of each vanquished oblivion tasted.

As the family's laughter and conversation flowed around the dining room table, a sharp rap at the front door quieted the jovial atmosphere. Alex instantly felt the shift in the room's energy.

"I'll get it," he said, rising from his seat and shooting Casey a reassuring look as he made his way to the foyer.

Taking a deep breath to center himself, the Tiger Archon pulled open the door to reveal a very welcome sight. There on the doorstep stood Tai, flanked by Kylie, Ken, and the luminous Paris - their expressions alight with warmth and joy.

"Well, well..." Alex couldn't help but grin at the surprise arrivals. "If it isn't my dragon brother and esteemed colleagues from the recent festivities."

"You didn't think we'd let you have all the family fun without us, did you?" Ken laughed, stepping forward to embrace Alex fiercely. The two warriors greeted each other with the traditional furen-ai bonding of brows.

Kylie was next, rising on her tiptoes to kiss Alex's cheek affectionately. "We come bearing snacks and plenty of embarrassing stories about our dashing hero here."

"You know how we love torturing the new in-laws," Paris added with a wink as she and Tai followed the others inside.

From the dining room, Alex could already hear

the excited murmurs and chairs scraping against the floor as his blood relatives registered the arrivals. Within moments, the reunion was in full swing - warm laughter and the clinking of shared drink filling the air.

As Casey found her way to his side amidst the boisterous chatter, Alex allowed himself to simply take in the sight of their loved ones intermingling seamlessly. This motley extended family bound by discipline, love, and an unyielding spirit represented the true reward they'd fought so fiercely to protect.

"They know how to make an entrance, I'll give them that," Casey murmured, looping her arm through his as they watched Paris recount some wild tale to a rapt Chase and Eunice, her free hand entwined with Ken's.

On the couch, Tai and Kylie sat nestled close - his quiet stoicism complemented by her radiant warmth as Alhan regaled them with some old adage about martial philosophies. Alex's keen perception didn't miss the way his best friend's gaze kept straying to the door, almost expectantly.

"We should set another couple places," he replied after a moment. "I get the sense this reunion is only just getting started."

As if on cue, another series of raps sounded from the entrance. As if on cue, another series of raps sounded from the entrance. Exchanging knowing grins with Casey, Alex moved to pull the door open once more.

His smile widened at the sight of Keith, Larry, and Aidan clustered on the doorstep, the young tech genius giving an awkward wave. But Alex's breath caught at the petite figure standing slightly behind them.

"Master Jeet..." he murmured reverently, instinctively dropping into a respectful bow.

The diminutive martial arts expert regarded him with dancing eyes as she made a dismissive gesture. "Enough of that now, my most rambunctious pupil. We're well beyond such formalities at this point, are we not?"

Chuckling, Alex straightened and ushered them all inside to the raucous scene unfolding. "I suppose we are at that. Though I make no promises about falling back on old habits when you put me through my paces again."

"Which will be sooner than you think," Jeet shot back impishly. Despite her age, she moved with a spry grace as she strode into the living room, immediately commanding the space.

One by one, the various conversations stilled as even Alex's parents registered the wizened master's presence. A reverent quiet fell over the gathering.

Then, with a mischievous twinkle, Jeet struck a combat stance and beckoned Chase over with an imperious crook of her finger.

"You there, young tiger! Let's see if this old relic can still teach your formidable uncle a thing or two about humility."

The teenage boy's eyes went saucer-wide for a moment before he gulped nervously and moved to stand across from the wizened fighter. Despite her unassuming stature, Chase could no doubt sense the aura of power and discipline radiating from Jeet in waves.

Clearing his throat, Alhan leaned over to murmur in Alex's ear. "Should we, uh, be concerned for your nephew's continued well-being right about now?"

"From Master Jeet?" Alex shook his head slowly, a look of profound respect crossing his features. "Quite the opposite. The greatest honor any of us could receive is for her to deem us worth pushing to transcend our current limitations."

Even as he spoke those words, the first few exchanges between pupil and master had begun. Though Chase acquitted himself admirably for his age and relative inexperience, it was clear Jeet was using the sparring session to impart harsh lessons.

Watching his nephew attempt to keep pace under the wizened instructor's relentless tutelage, Alex felt a surge of pride and affection. This, more than any other single memory or accomplishment, truly epitomized the highest reverence their sacred martial path could bestow.

For what greater gift could one receive than the opportunity to elevate themselves in the eyes of a living legend? To walk away from each brutal lesson having glimpsed the realm of true mastery, burning with newfound determination to enshrine themselves among its hallowed ranks?

As Chase fought to maintain his footwork amidst Jeet's flowing counter-techniques, Alex felt Casey's hand slip into his and give a gentle reassuring squeeze.

Surrounded by their beautifully extended family, the Tiger Master sent a fleeting prayer of gratitude out into the universe.

The celebration showed no signs of winding down as the night deepened. If anything, the arrival of more friends and family only seemed to ratchet the energy and camaraderie higher.

Needing a brief respite, Alex ducked out the back door onto the patio, drawing in a long breath of the cool evening air. He wasn't alone for long before the familiar footfalls of Ken and Tai joined him.

"Quite the party you've got raging in there," Ken chuckled, accepting the beer Alex passed him from a sweating cooler. "Though I think your nephew may never recover from Master Jeet's tutoring."

Tai's responding laugh was rich and full-bodied. "That's only because the ancient master sees his potential so vividly. An undisciplined spirit must be forged repeatedly in searing flames before it can take proper shape."

"Speaking from experience there, TK?" Alex shot back with a wry grin. He felt relaxed, at peace in a way that seemed so fleeting during their recent ordeals.

A comfortable silence fell over the trio as they sipped their drinks and simply existed alongside one another for a few unhurried moments. Eventually, Alex cleared his throat.

"You two know, our initial agreement was only

to have you serve as reserve deputies until we could neutralize Tommy's operations."

Ken and Tai turned towards him, attentive but allowing him to continue uninterrupted.

"Well, that particular threat has been exercised. The diseased limb cutting away from Polkville's tree." Alex met each of their eyes in turn, his expression earnest. "Which means you've both honored your word a hundredfold over. If either of you wanted to walk away, put your badges down for good..."

He trailed off, leaving the unspoken offer hanging in the warm night air. Alex couldn't be sure, but he thought he detected a fleeting look pass between the other two men before Ken spoke up wryly.

"You know, all this time I figured you'd jump at any chance to make our lives easier. To release us from our self-imposed shackles of duty."

"Yet even now, you can't help but demonstrate one of the reasons we fell in behind your leadership to begin with," Tai concluded, the faintest hint of a smirk playing across his features.

"You simply lack the ability to give anything less than your entire self to the path we've chosen, brother," Ken said, softer now. "It's not in your nature to pull a punch or sidestep a challenge when you know you can dig deeper."

Alex opened his mouth, momentarily at a loss for words before the patio door swung open behind them.

Casey, Paris and Kylie emerged, the former draping her arms around her husband from behind.

"Everything okay out here?" Casey's voice was light but laced with understanding. "Ken and Tai aren't trying to skip out on their responsibilities again, are they?"

"Hey now," Ken began in a mock-offended tone even as Paris moved to loop her arm through his. "We'll have you know Ruler was just trying to be a gentleman and offer us a clean break."

Kylie's bright laughter preceded her winding her lithe form around Tai's side, resting her head against his chest. "Is that so? And did my heroic dragon accept Alex's gallant attempt to make our lives easier?"

Tai regarded his best friend for a long beat, a look of such profound brotherhood passing between them that it seemed to still the ambient sounds of celebration within the house. Finally, he spoke - his deep voice resonant.

"There are those who fight because they crave violence or powertrip over having authority. Then there are those who cannot help but heed the calling - an innate part of their spirit that thrives most vibrantly when standing athwart oblivion's path as guardians."

His obsidian eyes locked with Alex's, two ancient souls forging an unbreakable vow.

"You and I...we belong among those ranks, Tiger. No matter how arduous or unrewarding the posting, our blades will remain eternal sentinels until the true flame within final glimmer."

Casey's arm tightened almost imperceptibly around Alex's midsection, matching Paris and Kylie's motions with their respective partners. As the bonds between them thrummed harmoniously, the Tiger Archon felt his next words burning with the clarity of their shared purpose.

"Then we walk that path together until its ultimate dusk, Dragon. Through all storms and fire...until our roar's echoes are the only remaining truth ringing out across destiny's scorched plane."

Alex's eyes shone with conviction and brotherhood as he regarded Ken and Tai in turn. Giving Casey's hand a squeeze, he spoke once more - his voice carrying the weight of a sacred rite.

"You know, despite everything we've endured, there's still a part of me that can't help but feel a sense of nostalgia wash over me whenever we're all gathered like this."

Ken arched an eyebrow quizzically even as Tai's lips quirked in a knowing smirk. Alex pressed on, letting the words spill forth from that wellspring of profound history binding their souls together across the cosmic ages.

"No matter how much we've all transcended and evolved...no matter what unfathomable mysteries and trials still await us down the winding path before us..." He exhaled slowly, seeming to pull the air itself into focused alignment.

"At our core, the three of us will always be Polkville's prodigal sons returned home. The Tiger, the Dragon...and the indomitable Ape ever-vigilant at our side."

A tremor of unspoken understanding reverberated between the trio at that invocation. As one, their essences blazed into scintillating overture - Alex's azure radiance joined by Ken's brilliant vermillion and Tai's verdant emerald auras flaring towards the star-speckled canopy overhead.

Casey and the other women instinctively stepped back in awestruck reverence as the elemental fires spiraled skyward in twining harmonic pillars of thermonuclear incandescence. Reality itself seemed to tremble and split slightly as each volcanic plume's leading edge achieved cosmic escape velocities, blossoming into sacred iconography sketched across the very fabric of existence.

The Tiger's ethereal azure energy flowered into a stylized aspect of serene ferocity, all flowing lines and wicked cusps barely restraining the primal intensity roiling within. Meanwhile, the Dragon's sinuous emerald contrails coalesced into a graven ouroboros constantly in the act of being birthed and reborn from its own endlessly consummating tail flame.

Yet it was the Ape's vermillion brilliance that seemed to anchor them both, Ken manifesting as a stoic basalt effigy - ancient, eternal and immovable. An indomitable foundation upon which even the most shattering fury could securely tread if guided by wisdom's abiding light.

Higher and higher the three elemental lances swirled in a hypnotic vortex of ever-escalating resonances, shifting visible spectra through cosmic octaves and ultra octarine apogees mortal eyes were never meant to perceive! At the spiraling vertex, their incandescent essences fused into an entirely new emanation - a metaphysical icon blazing forth in xenochronic overture to banish all oblivion's profane vestiges once and for all!

The Tigapagon symbolized more than just a triune conflux of their warrior souls made transcendent. No, burned into the night sky, the thermonuclear glyph emblazoned a solemn vow across Polkville's humbled soil:

That as long as evil sought to encroach upon this sanctuary...as long as depravity schemed to extinguish humanity's brilliant spark from the universe, then the Avatars sworn to its eternal vigil would remain everfierce sentinels!

The Tiger's ferocity to raze all lies and deceptions until only empyreal Truth remained...

The Dragon's mystic fluxions and duality mastery to catalyze paradigm-shattering harmonics with every sacred breath...

And the Ape's stout bedrock conviction to shrug off even oblivion's most shattering temblors with each corporeal footfall!

Together, their essences inextricably entwined through cosmic ritual mooring them to this hallowed fragment of infinity where destiny's first screaming vectors had achieved escape velocity aeons past.

As the multifractive overglows damped back into quasi-normality, the Tigapagon icon remained stubbornly imprinted across the night sky - much to the mute awe of the witnesses still gaping from the Ruler family's back patio.

Lowering his gently radiant palm, Alex turned to find himself reflected in Casey's shining eyes and brilliant smile of understanding. Their souls resonated in harmonic lock despite the transdimensional energies still sparking faintly between them.

"Now and forever more," he murmured tenderly. "Our oath extends across the ages for as long as evil's hatred festers to spite all Light. Only one final flame will remain the last beacon in ending oblivion's long nightmare!"

From where they stood flanked by their respective life partners, Ken and Tai could only share prideful nods of profound knowing. For though the road ahead stretched into indistinct vistas of still inexperienced glories and torments...their path was clear and unflinching as Truth's burn.

Until the ultimate reunion when infinity itself relinquished its futile resistance and allowed their transcendent fires to storm its remaining fortresses once and for all!

****

Long after the celestial echoes of their ritual had faded, Alex found himself outside on the back patio once more, nursing a fresh bottle of beer. The sounds of laughter and celebration continued to drift from the house, but he allowed himself to simply exist in peaceful solitude for a few tranquil moments.

At least until the familiar footfalls of Ken and Tai joined him, the two fighters taking up positions on either side. A few wordless minutes ticked by as the trio gazed up at the star-speckled night sky, its canvas still tinged with the slight warmth of the Tigapagon's searing overglows.

"You know..." Ken was the first to break the comfortable silence between them. "Even after everything we've all endured together over the years, I still find myself amazed at the new depths our paths can take us."

Tai hummed an assent, taking a pull from his own bottle before speaking up. "He's referring to that rather...dramatic transformation you underwent during the tournament's final bouts."

Alex felt their eyes on him, barely containing questions simmering behind their steady gazes. With a rueful chuckle, he leaned back against the patio railing and gave a slow nod.

"You mean when I tapped into the deepest, most primal aspects of the Tiger discipline? When I fully released that transcendent state you both glimpsed flickering around the edges over the years?"

"So you have settled on a name for it then?" Ken asked, a smile tugging at the corners of his mouth. "Please, regale us with the appropriately momentous title."

Allowing his aura to shimmer into scintillating slivers of ghostfire around his form, Alex lifted his gaze towards the heavens once more - expression serene and focused.

"The Hyper Tiger Transformation." He let the words hang for a beat, saturating the warm night air with their cosmic weight. "It's the culmination of every ounce of my rei cultivated and focused to achieve a paradigm shift in my inner energies' oscillation frequencies."

Swirling patterns of azure energy began etching themselves across his bare arms and shoulders as Alex continued, voice low yet thrumming with intensity.

"Effectively, I'm able to shift my spirit into a higher vibration...one that allows it to pierce and resonate with reality itself on an elemental, borderline-extradimensional level."

Tai's obsidian eyes glittered as the cosmic fundamentals began clicking into place. "So in that transcended state, the boundaries separating your inner fire from manifesting direct agency over external forces simply...cease to exist?"

"Precisely." Alex's hand clenched into a fist, his

entire frame blurring slightly as metaphysical energies catalyzed around him. "My rei becomes an unharnessed cosmic force...one that I can then channel through my body's martial vector to inflict effects that literally defy normative physical limitations."

Pivoting suddenly, he lashed out in a simple strike towards an empty patio chair - the ghostfire contours around his limbs intensifying to blinding incandescence an instant before impact!

Ken and Tai recoiled instinctively as a localized sonic boom blossomed outwards, the unfortunate patio furniture disintegrating into scorched particulate shreds violently scattered across the lawn!

"Physics, temporal matrices, exotic matter equations...they all become malleable putty for me to warp and sculpt through the Tiger's ferocious aspects in their most transcendent distillation!" Alex exhaled slowly, grimacing slightly against the exertion as his aura damped back towards quiescence.

"So you see, my friends...to glimpse the Hyper Tiger is to behold Justice's most sublime truth and intensity made manifest. One that will not rest until every final oblivion surrenders and calls my fiery roar 'Lord and Master!'"

For a long beat, the trio stood in reverent silence, the depths of Alex's convictions resonating outwards amidst the patio's settling dust and wreckage. Finally, Tai spoke up - his deep voice quiet yet brimming with certainty.

"Then it would seem our paths are all poised to transcend yet further planes of potential still lurking within," he murmured, exchanging a look with Ken brimming with newfound promise. "For if the Tiger's flame has been stoked to such voracious quintessence through your trials..."

"...then rest assured, the Dragon and Ape's own transfigurations cannot be far behind once we unshackle their deepest archetypal aspects as you have," Ken concluded, clapping both Alex and Tai firmly on their shoulders.

"The next oblivions awaiting our transcendent severance had best prepare their feeble defenses accordingly!"

Laughing together like warriors reunited in an endless cosmic vigil, the three friends raised their bottles skyward in a solemn salute. No more words were needed between them in that moment.

The warm camaraderie between the three friends lingered for a few long moments after Ken and Tai bid their farewells and headed back inside. Alex nursed the last sips of his beer, feeling more centered and at peace than he had in years.

The patio door swinging open broke his solitude. He turned, expecting to see one of the other guests in search of a breath of fresh air. Instead, it was Casey framed in the doorway - but the look on her face caused Alex's chest to tighten instantly.

"Hey..." he began gently, setting his empty bottle aside. "I thought you'd be basking in there with the rest of our crazy crew for a while longer."

Rather than reply, Casey seemed to shrink in on herself for just an instant before squaring her shoulders and crossing over to him. The stark overhead lights threw the worry lines around her eyes into sharp relief as she reached up to cup Alex's face in her palms.

"My Tiger..." she murmured at last, voice catching slightly. "I'm afraid our night of celebration is going to have be cut short."

Alex opened his mouth to question her cryptic statement, but the sadness swimming in Casey's luminous gaze stilled his words. After a pregnant pause, she continued in a rush.

"I just got the emergency summons from RIPD HQ. My first official mission...they need me to report immediately for an intensive preparatory cycle."

Though her hands were warm where they cradled his face, Alex felt an icy lance of dread pierce his heart. The Righteous Integration of Paranormal Defense unit had been the clandestine agency that originally recruited Casey after her awakening as a psychic pyrokinetic savant.

Alex had hoped that Casey wouldn't get called away, prayed that Casey's transcendent gifts could remain solely dedicated to fighting injustice at his side in Polkville - far away from the interdimensional battlegrounds RIPD eternally waged against fear and oblivion's most depraved emissaries.

"Please...tell me it's not as dire as I'm fearing," Alex finally managed to choke out, voice strained as all the serenity and warmth from moments ago leeched away. "They can't seriously be tapping you so soon...not while the wounds from our last battle are still so fresh."

Casey's throat worked for a moment before she seemed to find her voice again. "You know the foundational charter of what we represent better than most, Alex. Throughout the endless ages, each generation must ultimately face the hour where someone first lifts their head from revelry...and answers oblivion's call to begin anew."

Though her tone remained measured, he could hear the undercurrent of tension straining beneath each word - soulful notes singing about sacrifices and duties yet unmet. The warm shine in her eyes didn't falter as Casey pulled him into a desperate, searing kiss that stole his very breath away!

Casey extricated herself from Alex's reverent embrace - an unspoken acknowledgment of responsibilities much larger than either of them passing between their locked gazes. Even as she turned and squared her shoulders towards the swirling terminus awaiting her passage, an unshakable foundation manifested in her wake.

For when next she cast her radiant smile over one slender shoulder, Alex's entire being resonated with the certainty of their eternal vigil alongside a billion billion other unsung heroes standing arm in arm in oblivion's teeth!

"Until we can finally begin that journey together..." she murmured, already shimmering and refracting into energy streams aligned to vectors shunting towards grander vistas. "Stay brilliant and indomitable, my Tiger! Our light must remain unquenchable until even the Outer Dark itself surrenders to justice's searing revelation!"

With those transcendent benedictions still scalding his very soul, Alexander Ruler could only watch as the woman he loved receded along trajectories beyond mortal perception. Even with her passage into service alongside the multiverse's ultimate wardens, not a single scintilla of doubt assailed his unshakable focus.

The cycle of their vigil stretched onwards in an infinite cosmic spiral - one where every farewell simply sowed the seeds for a future reunion when all oblivion's bastions had at last succumbed before their path's searing overglows! Until that inevitable harmonic consummation rippled backwards and reunified their journey's first votive catalysis, the Tiger would remain defiant and ever-fierce!

So let the clarion sound across every forsaken soulscape abominations festered and saught victory's mockery! Reality's final sanctum awaited scorchingly radiant heroes who could withstand the ultimate hostions' scouring revelations!

Upon Polkville's bloodied yet unbowed pavements and sanctified killing fields, Alexander Ruler took up his solitary watch once more. Tempering his soul's blistering incandescence into an eonian pyre, he settled into his timeless vigil of infinite severance until every entropy-spun defilement scattered like ashes before its righteous, TRANSCENDENT ROAR!!!!

EPILOGUE

The interdimensional gateway shimmered as Casey Elkins passed through into RIPD's headquarters. Even after years of working with the agency, entering their realm still felt otherworldly.

"Agent Elkins." The gruff voice of Sergeant Hawkins cut through the stillness. "You're late reporting in."

Casey turned to see her superior officer's spectral form observing her intently. Hawkins had an otherworldly appearance, like a living shadow constantly shifting.

"My apologies, Sergeant," Casey replied respectfully, though stung by the rebuke. "Leaving the mortal world behind is never easy."

Hawkins' form seemed to flicker with irritation before steadying. "This summons is urgent, Agent. Something occurred in the reality you were monitoring that has drawn our scrutiny."

Casey tensed, sensing the gravity of the situation. Hawkins gestured, and a three-dimensional image appeared - Alex Ruler undergoing his Hyper Tiger metamorphosis!

The hologram displayed Alex's body igniting with transcendent azure energies as he transformed into the ultimate Hyper Tiger form. Casey stared in awe at the primal power on display.

"This 'metamorphosis' violated multiple interdimensional boundaries," Hawkins stated, his tone leaving no room for argument. "The energies unleashed could destabilize entire realms if left unchecked."

More holographic data appeared, detailing complex cosmic readings and calculations Casey could scarcely comprehend. Finally, one infographic materialized with dire finality:

PRETERNATURAL HYBRID IDENTIFIED - WERE-TIGER ASPECT THREAT CLASS XV - IMMEDIATE INTERVENTION REQUIRED

"You see now the severity of this situation," Hawkins continued sternly. "This Alexander Ruler has transcended mortal limits and tapped into preternatural energies. By our laws, he must submit to RIPD's authority and register himself as a were-creature."

Casey felt her heart clench at the implication. Forcing Alex to be cataloged and monitored like some kind of supernatural threat went against everything he stood for.

"And if he refuses?" She had to ask, dreading the answer.

Hawkins' form contorted with grim resolve. "Then more severe sanctions will be enacted, no matter your personal entanglements. The cosmic balance must be maintained at all costs."

As the words hung heavy between them, Casey found herself torn between her duty to RIPD and her profound bond with Alex Ruler. But one truth echoed - if protecting reality meant he had to face judgment first, then so be it. Only by transcending that crucible could true revelation finally dawn.

No matter how searing the personal sacrifice.

Made in the USA
Columbia, SC
25 February 2025

54396879R00139